Lean Fall Stand

D0823908

ALSO BY JON McGREGOR

The Reservoir Tapes
Reservoir 13
This Isn't the Sort of Thing That Happens to Someone Like You
Even the Dogs
So Many Ways to Begin
If Nobody Speaks of Remarkable Things

Lean Fall Stand

Jon McGregor

4th ESTATE • London

4th Estate
An imprint of HarperCollins*Publishers*
1 London Bridge Street
London SE1 9GF

www.4thEstate.co.uk

HarperCollins*Publishers*
1st Floor, Watermarque Building, Ringsend Road
Dublin 4, Ireland

First published in Great Britain in 2021 by 4th Estate

1

Copyright © Jon McGregor 2021

Jon McGregor asserts the moral right to be identified
as the author of this work in accordance with the
Copyright, Designs and Patents Act 1988

A catalogue record for this book is
available from the British Library

ISBN 978-0-00-820490-7 (hardback)
ISBN 978-0-00-820491-4 (trade paperback)

This novel is entirely a work of fiction. The names, characters
and incidents portrayed in it are the work of the author's imagination.
Any resemblance to actual persons, living or dead, events or
localities is entirely coincidental.

All rights reserved. No part of this publication may be
reproduced, stored in a retrieval system, or transmitted,
in any form or by any means, electronic, mechanical,
photocopying, recording or otherwise, without the
prior permission of the publishers.

This book is sold subject to the condition that it shall not, by
way of trade or otherwise, be lent, re-sold, hired out or otherwise
circulated without the publisher's prior consent in any form of
binding or cover other than that in which it is published and
without a similar condition including this condition being
imposed on the subsequent purchaser.

Set in Adobe Garamond Pro
Printed and bound in Great Britain by
CPI Group (UK) Ltd, Croydon

MIX
Paper from
responsible sources
FSC **FSC® C007454**
www.fsc.org

This book is produced from independently certified FSC™ paper
to ensure responsible forest management.

For more information visit: www.harpercollins.co.uk/green

To Rosie

LEAN /

1 /

When the storm came in it was unexpected and Thomas Myers was dropped to his knees.

The air darkened in the distance. There was a roar and everything went white against him. It had a kind of violence he wasn't prepared for. He wrapped his arms around his head and lay flat on the ice to keep from being hurled away.

His hand twitched instinctively towards his phone, although he knew there was no signal and his phone wasn't there.

His clothes felt as though they were being torn from his body, the air sucked from his lungs.

He had heard this described as like being inside a jet engine. As though people knew what being inside a jet engine was like. People said these things, but the words didn't always fit.

The roar of it was everything. He had only his weight against the ice to know which way up he was in the world. He couldn't see the others. He couldn't see anything.

The important thing was to stay calm, and take stock of the situation. Remember the training: find shelter or make shelter, remain in place, establish contact with other members of the party, keep moving, keep calm.

There were contradictions in the training.

It was difficult to think with the weather scouring wildly around him.

He didn't know where the radio was. He couldn't see the others. He needed to find his camera.

He had set up his camera tripod at the edge of the ice, trying to get a shot that foregrounded the still waters of the Sound with the cliffs of Priestley Head in the near distance. Luke had stayed with the skidoo and the rest of the kit. Ten, maybe fifteen metres to his left. Maybe more. Doc had gone off on the other skidoo and climbed up Priestley Head, to give the picture perspective. Without someone in the frame there was no way to capture the scale of this place. He'd been struggling with it since they'd first arrived. In the pictures he'd taken so far, everything looked too small. The distant mountains. The ridges on either side of the valley. The glacier. The icebergs creaking against each other, with the light turning bluely inside them. It was difficult to fit it all in.

He'd lined up a shot with Doc looking out from the cliffs of Priestley Head, scanning the waters. On the radio he'd told Doc where to stand; he must have put the radio down after that. Doc did a good polar explorer. He had the beard for it. The water was gleaming and grey and the mountains behind Doc were stark white against him. The auto-exposure kept jumping around. There was a shift in temperature. He'd glanced behind him and seen dark clouds banking over the top of Everard Glacier. He was just detaching the camera when the wind moved suddenly against him and he was dropped to his knees.

He must have put the radio down while he was adjusting the tripod. After speaking to Doc. He must have put it somewhere by his feet. It wouldn't be far.

The wind was too strong to stand up in, so he edged forwards on his elbows and knees. Forward and to the left. He called Luke's name, and heard nothing. He reached around for the radio. He edged a little further forward, and paused. The camera should be right there as well. He shouted for Luke again.

He wasn't frightened, yet. Luke wasn't far away. He was remaining calm. Retaining an awareness of his surroundings.

They had come down from the field hut by skidoo, down the bank from the plateau and across the skiway. The skidoos were parked a safe distance from the water. Doc had driven one to the foot of Priestley Head before climbing up to the cliffs. No more than ten minutes away. When the storm cleared, they would regroup.

He had left the camera bags with Luke, and walked towards the water, onto the ice. Ten metres. Twenty. No more. It was clean ice, and secure. The storm had come suddenly down from the top of Everard Glacier, behind them, to the south-east. He was crouching with his back to the wind. Luke should be with the skidoo and the bags away to his left. To his left and a little ahead. He shuffled in that direction, keeping his face away from the blast of the wind.

Remain calm. Stay in place. Make contact.

He shouldn't have put down the radio. He shouldn't have moved away from Luke. He shouldn't have agreed with Doc's idea about climbing Priestley Head just for the sake of a photograph. He'd let himself get distracted by the scenery. Doc kept pretending to be blasé about it, but it was hard not to just stop and stare. All that ice and snow and sea and sky. Glaciers and ridges and icebergs and scree. Weathering and wind-form and shear. The air so clear that distances shrank and all the colours shone.

The wind was still roaring around him. The cold was starting to seep through his clothes.

He thought he could hear the crackle of the radio but he couldn't be sure. The wind was still raw in his ears. He reared up on his knees and reached out into the blasting snow.

'Come in … K … K …'

'*Thomas, are ... come in.*'

It was Luke, barely. It seemed odd to hear him on the radio when he was so nearby.

He listened, and heard Luke's voice again. There were no clear words but he recognised the tone. He turned until he was facing the sound. The wind was hitting him to the left. He crouched very still and listened but he could only hear the wind. Being down on the ice like this was a mistake. Keep dry. Remain calm, stay in place, keep dry.

He eased to his feet, keeping his body low. The gusts came and went and he was knocked around. Buffeted. He took two steps with his hands held out in front of him. The snow blasted against his back. He heard Luke's voice again. It was behind him now. Something shifted in the quality of the sound and he saw open water at his feet. Roiling grey against the whiteness. Something was wrong. The water should have been behind him. He backed away. He was definitely starting to feel the cold.

He looked at the grey water and he concentrated. The wind was dropping slightly but it was still hitting the left side of his face. The wind must have changed direction. He turned through one hundred and eighty degrees, slowly.

He edged forwards with his hands held out.

There was the crackle of the radio again. Somewhere up ahead. He could hear Luke, asking Doc Wright to *come in, come in.* He crouched his way towards the sound. He wondered why Doc wasn't answering. He kept his steps slow and steady but he could feel his heart rate shooting up. He heard Luke's voice again. The sound was fainter now. There was a kind of ringing or rushing in his ears and he couldn't be sure he was hearing the radio at all. The wind bit against the right side of his face, and it hurt to open his eyes. He took three more steps and again he came to open water. He watched it slosh against the edge of the ice. The sound of the radio had gone.

He was doing this all wrong. He should have stayed in place when the storm hit. He should never have moved. He could be close to Luke and the skidoo or he could have lost them altogether. Luke could have gone off in the wrong direction, looking for him. He should have stayed where he would know his location when the storm lifted. He should have stayed where he could have been found. He shouted Luke's name again. His voice was nothing against the storm.

He kept moving to keep himself warm. The noise of the wind made it hard to think clearly. The radio was behind him now. He could feel the chill beginning to bite. The air felt raw and violent.

The number of calories they got through in a day, down here. It was hard work just eating enough food.

He heard the radio again, and again he scrabbled around at his feet. Luke's voice was shrill, and distant. There were breaks in the transmission. '*Doc, Thomas, come in. Come in, Doc?* [...] *anyone?* [...]'

There would be food at the skidoo, when he found Luke. The dark grey water sloshed against the edge of the ice. The weather was thick and he could barely stand straight. He felt dizzy. Unsteady. Almost seasick.

Something was wrong.

2 /

'Doc, Thomas, come in. Come in, Doc? Hello, anyone? Over?'

From the low shelter of the skidoo, Luke Adebayo listened, again, for a response. It was too soon to be worried, but he should have heard something by now. He was getting cold already. He checked the battery levels and the volume, tucked the handset back inside his jacket, and ran through his options.

He could stay put. The training had been ambiguous on this point. They'd been told to stay put in bad weather, to avoid the risk of getting lost. But they'd also been told to find any shelter they could, and to make contact. If he couldn't make contact or find shelter, the case for staying put seemed weak.

He shouted into the wind, and nothing came back.

This was brutal. He could try and find Thomas, and they could both go and look for Doc together. Thomas had been close to the water when the storm came in, and if he'd wandered too far he'd be in danger. He was the priority. Doc had the experience to do the right thing. But neither of them were responding. Luke could barely see his hand in front of his face. It was too much of a risk. He didn't want to start wandering off in circles.

If the two of them were lost he would need outside help, which would mean getting back to the field hut and radioing from there. It had taken less than twenty minutes to get here on the skidoo, and it shouldn't take much more to get back. If he could stick to the right bearing, in these conditions. The field hut was bang centre on the plateau beneath Garrard Ridge. It was bright red, also. It shouldn't be too hard to miss. But nothing was too hard to miss in this weather.

They weren't lost. They couldn't be lost. They were out of radio contact for a time, was all. The best thing would be to stay in place until he heard from them.

They shouldn't have split up like that, in any case. Doc was always saying he knew this place like the back of his hand but they were still literally in the middle of nowhere. Going off for a photo opportunity had seemed suboptimal. Luke had thought it was a bad idea as soon as Doc suggested it. Thomas had just made a face like: no point arguing with the man, might as well get it over and done with. Get back to the hut for another night of hot chocolate and charades and listening to Doc's stories.

People were going to ask him a lot of questions about Antarctica, when he got home, and one thing he wouldn't be able to tell them was that a lot of the time it was pure boring. Beautiful, yes. Awe-inspiring and majestic or humbling or whatever else you wanted to call it, but once you were done looking, the actual experience of being here day after day was kind of long.

He edged out from behind the skidoo and called Thomas's name again. He could barely hear himself, let alone any possible reply. He ducked back down. He wondered if it was too soon for emergency rations. He cleared the snow from his glasses and tried the radio again. It occurred to him that perhaps they just couldn't hear their radios, with the noise of the storm.

There would certainly be a discussion about all this tonight. He suspected that not all of it would get back to Main Base. Doc had mentioned several times that he didn't do everything by the book. Luke didn't really know what to make of the man. They'd been down at Station K. for three weeks, and Luke was still trying to figure him out. At the training conference no one had taken him that seriously. There were jokes made behind his back. It was easy to wind him up and he didn't always notice. He was strict about the logbook and the radio schedule, and what he called *keeping a tight ship*, but he was relaxed about other things. How much they drank, for example. He started drinking pretty early in the day. But he'd been working as a technical assistant down here for thirty-odd years and he obviously knew his stuff. He would know how to get them out of a difficult situation.

The wind showed no sign of dropping. It was constant and roaring. He tried the radio again.

'Thomas, Thomas, come in? Doc, come in? Over.'

He waited, with the handset pressed up against his ear. There was a hiss of white noise. He tried not to think about how far they were from Main Base, or from any other human activity

12

whatsoever. The Russian base was probably the closest, and that was at least a day by skidoo.

'Thomas, Thomas, come in? Doc, come in? Over.'

There was another hiss, and the faint crackle of an incoming transmission. And then nothing.

'Thomas, Thomas, come in? Doc, come in? This is Luke, this is Luke. Over.'

'... *is Thomas, this is Thomas. Over.*'

'Nice one, Thomas, thank fuck. You were starting to worry me, where the fuck are you? I can't see you. I can't see anything.'

'*Yes, Luke ... issue, over.*'

'Missing word before issue, can you repeat, over?'

'... *find the radio. That problem's over, over.*'

'Yeah, okay, okay. Have you heard from Doc? Over.'

'*Negative, over.*'

'Maybe we should get over to the Head and find him, what do you think? Over.'

'... *broken, can you repeat, over?*'

'Can you hear me now? Should we go and find Doc? Where are you?'

'... *this ... again ... out.*'

The wind dropped for a moment and then slammed into him again. The visibility was still close to zero. Thomas must surely be close by. He'd been right over there when the storm hit. No distance at all. They should regain contact. Wait for the weather to clear. He wondered what was wrong with Doc's radio. Or with Doc. Thomas was obviously wondering the same.

'*Doc, Doc ... Come in ... Doc? Over.*'

It was probably just a technical issue. It would be resolved soon enough. Knowing Doc, there was always the chance this was some kind of test, or weird joke. He could be listening to them both now.

'Doc, Doc ... Come in ... Doc? Over.'

3 /

Robert 'Doc' Wright had seen the storm coming, but there had been no time to warn the others.

The afternoon had been given over to recreational activity, once the team completed their GPS survey activities. They had set out from the Station K. field hut at 1300 hours, travelling down to the shoreline by skidoo, with the principal intention of facilitating Thomas's photography interests. A suggestion had been made that he provide some human scale to Thomas's shots by ascending Priestley Head, a short distance away. This was pushing at the bounds of correct operating procedure but it didn't seem unreasonable. Conditions were excellent, and it wasn't far. He'd maintained visual and radio contact at all times. From the top of the Head he'd provided Thomas with the necessary postures for his photographs.

Priestley Head was little more than a bump in the topography, really. It had taken five minutes to walk up from where he'd left the skidoo; the cliffs facing out to the Sound were barely thirty metres above the water. Enough to add a little drama to Thomas's pictures. From here the view of the whole valley was excellent. In the near distance, the red field hut of Station K., sheltered in the lee of Garrard Ridge and the peaks of K7 and K8 beyond. Below the field hut, the ground sloping down to the skiway, marked by orange fuel drums and black flags, and beyond that the dark grey waters of Lopez Sound, fringed with fast-ice. In the Sound the icebergs had turned against each other, dipping and rocking with a sudden unexpected movement in the water. Doc had looked up towards Everard Glacier and seen a thick rolling shadow of banked clouds, a faint orange light, a surge of weather coming down towards them. It had come out of nowhere and it had come in fast, the temperature dropping sharply. He'd seen Thomas glancing over his shoulder and trying to fold away his camera tripod, and when he'd tried the radio there'd been no response. He'd seen Luke standing beside the skidoo, turning to look at him. He'd barely managed two steps towards the shelter of the slope before the wind slammed hard against him and pushed him back towards the edge of the cliff.

He adopted a prone position, slipping quickly across the loose scree, scrabbling for a foothold and finding only thin air behind him. He stretched out his arms and tried to shift his weight forward. He closed his eyes and concentrated. He arched one foot out and around to the left, bringing his knee up towards his chest. The noise of the wind was so violent it was difficult to think. His boot touched rock, finally, but when he pushed out against it the rock loosened and fell down the sheer drop. For a long giddy moment his weight swayed away after it.

He slowed his breathing. He concentrated. He inched his way forward again. The cliff wasn't high but he wouldn't survive a fall.

His hands felt loose inside his gloves. The scree felt slippery beneath him. He could feel the edge of the ridge against his waist, his legs hanging in the air. He pressed himself flatter against the rock, working his weight further forwards. His radio was in his inside jacket pocket, and crushing against his ribs. He felt it vibrate. The other two would be checking in now, surely. He had no way to respond. He trusted them not to panic. They would shelter in place, as per the training.

He had been in these situations before. This was no different. You didn't go thirty-odd seasons on the ice without getting into one or two scrapes. The trick was to slow down and start thinking. Always have the next step in mind. His next step here, obviously, would be to transfer his weight forward and roll clear of the edge, before moving down into shelter and making contact with his colleagues. He took several slow breaths, and made an effort to rationalise his thoughts. He flexed his fingers to maintain the circulation. You won't fall until you let go, a supervisor had told him once, during crevasse training. The logic wasn't entirely sound but the spirit was a fine one. Don't look down; don't let go. Hold on. The trick was to hold on, always.

4 /

Thomas walked into the camera tripod and fell to his knees. The camera was still attached. He heard the radio crackling, and found it lying in the snow.

'Hello, hello, this is Thomas, this is Thomas, over.'

There was a long pause. He held the radio against his ear, and listened to the hissing against the howl of the wind.

'Nice one, Thomas, thank fuck. You were starting to worry me, where the fuck are you? I can't see you. I can't see anything.'

'Yes, Luke. Having a temporary navigational issue, over.'

'... issue, can you repeat, over?'

'I couldn't find the radio. That problem's over, over.'

'Yeah, okay, okay. Have you heard from Doc? Over.'

'Negative, over.'

'Maybe ... should ... Head ...'

'Your transmission is broken, can you repeat, over?'

'... hear me now? ... find Doc ...'

'Luke, I'm not getting this. I'll try again in a bit. Over and out.'

He could feel the lack of sugar in his blood. It made him feel cottony and soft. He brushed the snow off the camera and tried turning it on, but nothing happened. It had been a present from his girlfriend. He knew how much she'd spent. He found an energy bar in his pocket, and tried to eat steadily, so as not to cramp his stomach. He thought about the flask of coffee that Luke had packed on the back of the skidoo. They made their coffee with a lot of sugar and hot chocolate down here. The wind dropped for a split second then gusted back to full force. It would surely clear soon enough. He felt the adrenalin fade. These little dramas were always short-lived. It wasn't like the old days, Doc kept telling them, and Thomas was glad about that.

When he'd told people he was going to Antarctica it had sounded dramatic, but it really wasn't that big a deal. He'd been climbing in the Alps and the Pyrenees with far less technical support than they had here. They were in regular contact with the main base at Bluff Point, and the skiway meant that assistance was a few hours away at most. Doc kept telling them how utterly self-reliant they had to be down here, but Thomas hadn't really bought it.

The cold was gnawing into him now. His hands and feet were starting to feel numb. He jogged on the spot to get the blood moving again through his body. He stuffed the camera inside his jacket to try and warm it up. Sophie had been so pleased with herself when she gave it to him. She kept checking that she'd chosen the right one. His arms and legs felt stiff with tension. The radio crackled again, and he heard Luke still trying to reach Doc.

19

He asked Luke for his current location, and Luke said he was still with the skidoo, he hadn't gone anywhere, and where was Thomas though? The signal was clearer, briefly. He asked Luke what he thought they should do.

He had lost faith in his sense of direction. He had a handheld GPS in his jacket, and he fired it up without really knowing how it would help. Getting off the ice and up the bank would be a start. This storm would blow itself out soon. Or it wouldn't. A storm like this could last for hours. The GPS unit was having trouble calibrating. He wasn't thinking straight. He started to radio an approximation of his current position through to Luke, but the lat and long figures kept shifting. He tried turning it off and on again. He had that seasick feeling again.

There was still no word from Doc. It would be ironic if he'd let his radio go flat. He was always talking about the importance of good radio discipline: checking the batteries, maintaining the handsets, keeping communications to a minimum. He was a *stickler* for it. He'd actually used that word. I'm a stickler for this, boys, I'm afraid. He was a stickler for everything, basically. He had a thing about the daily routine, and about keeping the hut shipshape, and about inspecting the stores. He had a blind spot with the satellite phones, apparently, and had managed to run them flat overnight. It wasn't the first time they'd had to leave them at the field hut. But Doc insisted they were less reliable than the radio in any case.

The numbers on the GPS unit kept changing. It made no sense. Luke came back on the radio and said they could both take a bearing and walk exactly towards each other. Thomas told him to stay with the skidoo, for fuck's sake.

He ate the last of his energy bar, and tried calling Doc again.

'Doc, Doc, come in? This is Thomas, this is Thomas, come in? Can you confirm a plan of action, confirm plan of action? Over.'

There was a burst of white noise from the handset, and then silence. The silence was the wind suddenly dropping. The effect of it still roared in his ears. As the wind faded, the visibility lifted. The sunlight moved hard against the water in all directions. He saw Luke, in the distance. The problem was immediately clear. The wind came rushing back in again and everything went dark.

5 /

'Doc, Doc, come in? This is ... this is Thomas, come in? Can you confirm ... action? Over.'

Luke listened to Thomas on the radio. There was still no response from Doc. If this was a wind-up it wasn't that funny. More likely he had some technical issue. He was probably waiting for the weather to clear, and then would expect them all to make their own way back to the hut. Luke could imagine him standing in the doorway of the storm porch, waiting for them. Making a face, like: *what time do you call this, lads?*

He'd made that face the first time they'd met him, at the training conference. Luke and Thomas had gone out in the evening for a drink, a couple of miles down the road to the local village. It had been dark when they'd left, and it took longer to get back than they'd expected. When they got to the conference centre the main door was locked, and while they were working out what to do, Doc Wright had come down and let them in. They introduced themselves and told him they'd taken a wrong turn. He asked what department they were in. Geographic

Information Systems, they said. He nodded. *Making a good start, lads.*

The training conference was run out of a ski lodge, north of Aviemore. Nearly a hundred of them bunked up in there. Long mornings in the dining hall sitting through lectures and PowerPoint presentations, and afternoons doing sledge hauling and kit testing and first aid. Luke hadn't known anyone when he arrived. It was like the first day of university all over again. People asking each other what their field was, and where they were from, and whether they'd been to Antarctica before. A hierarchy soon emerged. The ones who had been South dropped acronyms into conversation, and made a show of looking bored during lectures, and said things like *it's when you don't feel the cold that you really need to worry.* The first-timers stuck together and pretended to know things already. He met Thomas on the second day, when they were paired up to practise tying splints and wrapping plaster casts. Luke had never thought of plaster casts as part of first aid, but the instructor pointed out that in the field they would be away from medical professionals for weeks at a time. You might need to carry out an appendectomy with a doctor on the other end of a radio, she said. Luke had given Thomas a look to say: *mate, you're not touching my fucking appendix,* and they'd had trouble taking the rest of the session seriously.

After the first aid they were shown the recorded deaths. There were several slides. It was a long list. Navigational errors, hypothermia, climbing accidents, crevasse falls, drownings, incidents in which alcohol was noted as a factor, carbon monoxide poisoning, attack by seals, cardiac arrests, fire. Luke didn't mention any of these things to his parents. Thomas had been bothered by the ones listed as MISSING (PRESUMED DEAD). He wanted to know who had done the *pre*suming, and when it had become *as*suming.

The lists had made Luke think of Wile E. Coyote from the Road Runner cartoons, being endlessly crushed and dropped and blown apart with dynamite, and coming back for more. It was the 'attack by seals' that really set him off. Like, how were you not going to outrun a seal?

He hadn't seen Thomas again until they got to the airport, on their way to Antarctica. All the Institute people had been booked on the same flight, and the departure hall was full of their bright yellow kitbags and branded burgundy fleeces. There was more facial hair than there had been in Aviemore, and a lot of loud voices. When Thomas came over to say hello, Luke asked how on earth he'd spotted him in this crowd. *It must be the glasses*, Thomas had said, deadpan.

It took nearly a week of travelling to get to the main research base, most of it on a ship that actually crunched through solid ice in a way everyone pretended was no big deal. When they arrived they went straight into another two days of training, and this time they listened to every word. They were lowered into a crevasse and shown how to climb out; they stretchered a casualty down a cliff edge; they were dropped into the water and pulled out again. The importance of paying close attention to weather forecasts and scheduled radio transmissions was made clear, and those who had been there before said things like *once the toe turns black you're better off amputating before it spreads*. There was

24

another week of field training, and of preparing all the kit for their flight down to Station K., and then they were off.

There was no way of knowing how long this storm would go on for. They needed a plan. Thomas needed to get back up here from the ice. The two of them together could go and find Doc, or return to the field hut and use the HF radio to call Main Base.

There was a strange ringing sound in his ears, and it took a moment to realise that the wind had stopped. The sun burned suddenly through the blowing snow, and he stood up from behind the skidoo.

Thomas was fifty or sixty metres away. It was hard to judge. He was standing on the ice, looking at Luke. There was clear grey water between them. He didn't understand what he was looking at. There had been movement of some sort. Something had happened. The storm must have disrupted the ice. Something was wrong.

They looked at each other. The wind came roaring back, and Thomas disappeared from view.

Thomas's voice came back on the radio, shouting above the renewed force of the wind.

'*Luke, you saw? You saw? I'm moving. I'm on an ice floe, I'm fucking adrift.*'

'Say again? Adrift? Over.'

'*Repeat. I am on an ice floe, drifting across Lopez Sound. You fucking read me? Over.*'

'Thomas, what? What? Confirm? You can't be drifting. It must be a tide crack. Work around it? Find your way, I mean. Thomas?'
'*Luke, I've got the GPS running. I'm drifting. For real.*'

Luke put his helmet on and got the skidoo started. He had to get back to the field hut and contact Main Base. He had to find Doc and make sure Doc was okay. He had to find his way through the storm.

6 /

Doc Wright tried to slow his breathing. He concentrated on keeping the weight forwards, on his arms. He heard the faint crackle of his radio, and felt the vibration of it against his ribs. There was a shrill hiss of white noise, like the sound of applause, almost indistinguishable from the wind.

'... *the bay. Heading north-north-east, repeat, heading north-north-east.*'

Even in his precarious position Doc was able to be furious. He couldn't see why Thomas had decided to move in a north-north-east direction, away from his previous location. He couldn't picture where he might be that he could even head that way. If he'd moved from his position at all it should have been to regain contact with Luke. He would have to run over these things with the pair of them once they were back at the hut.

He groped around with his foot again, and finally found a hold that felt secure. He pushed gently against it and wriggled his way forward across the scree. There was very little strength left in his arms. When he was far enough from the edge he rolled onto his back and reached for the radio. Move to safety. Make contact.

'Thomas? Luke? Come in? This is Doc. Hello, hello. Thomas? Luke? Hello? Come in? Over.'

He waited. There was nothing but white noise. The wind was fierce and showed no sign of dropping. He tried the radio again. Persistence was important. He became aware of a trembling in his arms and legs, and a kind of vibration in his chest. He was familiar with the effects of adrenalin on the body. Shaking was one. Elevated pulse. Laboured breathing. There was an interaction of adrenalin with hypothermic symptoms.

He crawled forward, keeping low across the scree and ice until he could move down to the slope. He edged into a shallow scoop in the rock, turning his back on the wind. There was a slight drop in volume. He waited. He tried the radio again. He needed a plan, obviously. He was shaking. Christ. That was a close call.

It wasn't far to fall but the odds would have been slim. The shock of the cold water would have done for him, if nothing else. Would barely have been time to know what was going on.

No need to dwell. Important to concentrate on the matter at hand. He massaged the muscles in each arm, trying to work the adrenalin loose and regain some feeling. There was a peculiar stiffness in his neck. He could feel his temperature falling. At

1500 hours another series of transmissions came through on the radio.

'*Doc, come in, hello? Require assistance, repeat, require assistance. Immediate ... Doc ... Over.*'

He attempted a response but was unable to press the transmit button on his handset. This was; he would call this an escalation in the situation. He made the decision to get back to the skidoo and return to base. It was a calculated risk, in the circumstances, but he knew from experience that calculated risks were an integral part of field operations in Antarctica. A good technical assistant had to know when to take risks. He stood, bracing himself against the wind and preparing for the descent. The radio crackled again. There was a rattle of broken white noise, and snatches of Thomas's voice.

'*... location. Repeat ... visual confirm ...*'
'*... fucking what ... broke ... over.*'
'*Repeat your transmission? Over.*'

He waited, and listened, but there was nothing more. He pushed out from behind the shelter of the rock. Priestley Head was a narrow formation, and he would only have to follow gravity to regain the skidoo. He would talk to those two about radio discipline later.

He planted his feet and kept his weight low and leaned into the wind. He felt his way back down the slope, one careful step at a time. Now that he was moving, the stiffness was fading. The roar of the wind was dropping away. As he moved he felt the blood easing back into his fingers. He tried the radio again.

'Thomas, Luke, come in? This is Doc. I am returning to base, returning to base, over.'

He waited, and listened, and nothing came back.

After a few minutes of careful descent, he found his way to the skidoo. The snow was banked up against the windward side of it, and he grabbed the shovel to dig it out.

Thomas's voice came over the radio again. The lad was going to have to think about conserving his batteries.

'*Okay, this is Thomas. I'm going to try and work my way back, over.*'

Doc got on the radio, and started to ask Thomas to confirm his location. Something sharp struck him on the back of the neck and he went down fast.

7 /

'Stand by for updated coordinates, over.'

The Sound was two miles wide at this point, but beyond Priestley Head it narrowed and dog-legged to the east before widening to the open sea. If the wind kept up he could be blown against the shore past Priestley Head. If the floe kept moving. If the floe stayed intact. He thought back to the training. The phrase *floe-hop* came to mind. If he could find his way across. He knew now that the wind was coming from the south, from the glacier, so he had to move to the west, to his left, towards the land. When he moved he felt unsteady. He got down on his knees and shuffled in that direction. He saw water sloshing against the edge of the ice. There were pieces breaking off. He shuffled back again.

Luke was on the radio, saying something about Doc. The signals were weak, and interrupted.

'Luke, repeat that? I need some help here, Luke?'
'... *Doc. On Priestley Head. Stay calm, mate. Stay where ...*'
'Luke? Are you with Doc? What's the plan?'
'... *get help. Repeat, will get help. Stay calm, over.*'

The wind was unrelenting, but the sound of the water against the fractured edges of the ice was suddenly very loud. He remembered something from the training about searching in squares. Moving downwind, and across, and back. If he could find an adjacent floe, and move across to it, he could keep moving that way to the land. He worked forwards again, and away to the right. A few shuffling movements at a time. Keeping his head low, out of the wind. He could feel the cold clawing through him. He came to a crack in the ice. It wasn't a crack. The two sides of the crack were sliding against each other. This was another floe. He could move across. As he shuffled closer the gap started to widen.

There was no need for panic. The current direction of drift would take him to land just past Priestley Head. They would be able to pick him up. The Twin Otter could get down from the main base at Bluff Point in a matter of hours. They would bring the necessary equipment. Doc Wright would pass on the information and a plan would be made. This wasn't the old days, where they'd all had to fend for themselves.

There was a movement in the water. A shadow or a turning over of a wave.

He was starting to feel the cold. He backed away from the water and shuffled up and down on the spot. He couldn't hear himself think. It was important to keep the blood circulating, but it was also important to conserve energy. There were these inconsistencies in the training. He went through his pockets and found another energy bar that he'd stashed away a few days ago. It took all his concentration to bite off the end of the wrapper.

When he told Sophie about all this, later, she would pick up on how much they'd been eating. She'd be shocked by how much sugar and chocolate he was putting in everything down here. How much he was eating in general. She didn't take sugar in her tea, or even milk. She snatched out the teabag almost as soon as she'd put it in. It was a very thin kind of drink, the way she made it. It wasn't that she watched her weight; she just had an appetite for the clean and simple. He'd even seen her drink plain boiled water, sometimes. His mother had talked of nothing else, the first time he'd brought Sophie home. *I'll just have some hot water, thanks.* The look on his mum's face. What an introduction. Was she a ballet dancer or what, his mum had wanted to know, later. *Hot water?*

'*Doc, come in, Doc? The fuck are you? Doc?*

'…'

'*Thomas, I don't think … Doc's not here. The skidoo. His skidoo's gone. His helmet's here, but … I need to … the field hut. Stay calm, stay calm, over.*'

'Luke? Come in, come in? Luke? Where are you now? Have you called Main Base, over?'

There was only white noise from the handset when he pressed it against his ear. The battery warning light was starting to flicker. He switched it to low-power mode. He just had to be patient. He had to stay calm.

33

His parents had liked Sophie, despite the hot water thing. *They said you were nice*, he told her, in bed. She'd punched his shoulder because she couldn't believe they'd said something so bland. *Believe me*, he'd said. *They don't often have an opinion about anything. You're doing well.* Distracted by the fit of her body against his. The hardness of her. The way her muscles twisted densely beneath her skin as she shifted position around him. He'd seen her hanging from a hold by one hand, at the climbing wall. The concentration in her eyes. Not thinking about that move, but the one after that and the one after that. Her shoulder blades shifting beneath her T-shirt as she slowly shifted her weight. It was a kind of dance. He liked to watch her but he didn't go to the climbing centre often. The men there made him have doubts. They had handshakes that could crush cans. They all knew Sophie by name. Climbing wasn't his thing. Beside her in bed his body felt soft and loose.

He should be thinking about his next move, and the one after that. If he reached land beyond Priestley Head and the others weren't there to meet him. If the wind pushed him in a different direction. If the radio failed.

He was feeling the cold and he couldn't remember if that was a good thing or a bad thing. The wind was still scouring against him, but the visibility was starting to lift. There was less snow blowing out here on the water. He could see other ice floes. There was a lot of movement. He could see the dark water, churning. Something broke the surface of the water nearby. A dark head and a long smooth back. It twisted across the surface and disappeared.

Doc would have spoken to Main Base by now. Even without the satphones. He would have gone back to the hut and got on the HF radio. He definitely had an attitude about using the satellite phones. As if they were cheating in some way. But the radio would still get through.

There was a movement in the water, and the wind hit with renewed force. He crouched lower with his back to it, pulling his hood further over his head. This was good, in a way. This wind would get him to land sooner. As long as the floe didn't break up. As long as the wind didn't change direction.

He was feeling the cold and he couldn't remember the plan.

He needed a plan. He needed to know his next move.

The leopard seal has a distinctive look, the trainer had said. Long and narrow. A bullish head. This one had only surfaced twice but Thomas was sure it was still there. *Circling* would be too strong a word. It was maintaining a presence.

He remembered the way the sky had changed colour, just before the storm hit. The bright sunshine before that. How quickly things could change. The polished blue sky behind the head of the glacier turning a murky orange-brown. Darker. Blackening. The light going out. The weather gathered over the ridge.

The leopard seal was still there. Surfacing; slipping away.

He crouched into a tight huddle and he wasn't cold.

If he had to swim he wondered how far he would get.

He could swim back to the shore and radio Main Base for himself. But how would he get to the hut, and where was the skidoo, and what if the radio got wet? But these were not those circumstances.

Nobody could swim in this water. He stayed calm. He sat tight.

The radio crackled into life, and Doc Wright told him to stand by.

'*Stand by for a brief quickening,*' Doc said. '*Situation upstate.*'

8 /

The flight to Station K. had been so loud it made Luke feel sick. He spent most of the journey looking out of the window, trying to keep his breakfast down. The roaring white noise of the engines and the rattle of the thin fuselage cut right into him. There were bits of him vibrating that shouldn't have been vibrating at all.

Doc Wright kept trying to tell them things, but his words weren't getting through. He was sitting next to the pilot, and he kept slipping out of his seat belt to lean round towards Luke or Thomas, shouting towards their ears. Each time Luke nodded in vague agreement and turned back to the small window beside his seat.

He had studied the maps of this whole coastline, and especially of the area around Station K. where they would be working, but the maps and the aerial photographs hadn't really been enough to prepare him. The distances were immense, and featureless.

Actually *featureless* didn't quite describe it; there were mountains, and ridges, and slopes of scree, and glaciers moving down into inlets and sounds. But without trees, or rivers, or buildings, it was difficult to arrange what he was seeing into any kind of perspective. There was no obvious difference between one mile and fifty.

Thomas was busy with his camera, swapping lenses, trying to find a perspective that would make any sense on the screen. The pilot was talking on the radio occasionally, looking at dials, flicking switches, making adjustments on a touchscreen, pointing things out to Doc.

The rear of the plane where they were sitting was mostly taken up with supplies. The seats, pressed up against the open cockpit, seemed almost an afterthought. There were bolts and hooks on the ribbed steel floor. The fuselage was in jointed sections, and from where he was sitting he could touch the bolts holding two of the sections together. The bolts were very small.

Doc turned around again, and shouted something towards Thomas's ear. Thomas turned to Luke and shouted the message on.

'HE SAYS IT'S DOWN THERE.'

'WHAT?'

'DOWN THERE. HE SAYS IT'S THERE.'

'WHAT IS?'

'STATION K.'

'WHERE?'

'THERE. NEAR THE BAY. RED BUILDING. SEE?'

Doc was watching them, expectantly. Luke looked at him and shook his head. He thought he could see a scrap of rust against the snow, but it disappeared when he blinked. The roaring of the engines changed pitch. From the window Luke could see the elevations begin to match up with the contour lines they'd been studying, and the smudge of rust resolve itself into a small red building with a black roof. Down towards the water there was a faint streak that soon became two dotted lines, and as the mountains gained sudden height on either side of them he could see clearly the shapes of the field hut, the stores, the fuel dump, the long still stretch of water in the Lopez Sound and the flags marking out the skiway, the pilot muttering checks to herself and watching the dials and lights, making constant small adjustments, the white noise roar getting louder and more urgent and Luke braced back in his seat as the flaps were dropped and the engines changed pitch again, and now the line of Garrard Ridge was clear to their right, rising to the K7 and K8 peaks beyond, the land becoming very three-dimensional and solid and several icebergs catching the light in the water to their left and the whiteness rushing up to meet them and the skis jolting and shuddering and shaking across the packed snow. A white spray flew past the windows. The pilot was saying something to Doc, the controls juddering in her hands as she brought the plane almost to a standstill.

Doc turned back to them and smiled, with a mixture of what looked like pride and excitement. Thomas pressed his camera to the window and took more pictures. Outside, as the plane turned and taxied back, they could see three figures in bright red overalls, waiting for them at the midpoint of the skiway. It was a shock to see anyone out there. They were leaning against several stacks of crates, fuel drums, and waste barrels. They looked like men on a cigarette break behind a warehouse; conserving their movements, talking from the sides of their mouths. They watched the plane without moving, as if they'd seen all this before.

Doc was shouting something to him again, but Luke still couldn't hear a word. He nodded, and smiled. The plane came to a stop with a slight jerk, and Thomas banged his face against the window.

They unstrapped and opened the doors. The light flooded in and Luke swapped his glasses for sunglasses. They climbed out, jumping a short distance from the steps to the ice. Luke wanted to make a joke about a small step for mankind but he couldn't work out how to phrase it. The pilot kept the engines running. It wasn't as cold as Luke had expected. There was a dampness in the air. The three men waited, and Doc went over to shake their hands. For a moment it looked as though he might salute. Luke turned to Thomas and mimed smacking his face against glass. Thomas mimed telling him to *fuck off*.

They unloaded the stores from the hold, working quickly, passing the crates from hand to hand. Luke liked the sound of it: *unloading the stores from the hold*. Some of the supplies were in wooden sledge-crates that looked like they'd been around since the 1950s, with stencilled labels and crossed-out dates. *Theod. Comps. Tools, ass. Manfood.* They built a stack of crates to the side of the skiway, along with the fuel drums and empty waste barrels. The team they were replacing didn't have much to say. Luke paused for a moment to rearrange the stack of crates, and when Thomas came back he made it look as if he were struggling.

'Thomas?'

'Luke.'

'Can you give me a hand with these tools, ass?'

'Lol out loud, mate.'

They helped the outgoing team load the cases and empty fuel barrels that were going back to Bluff Point. The pilot was very particular about what went where, and how it was strapped down. Luke was building up heat already, and had to unzip his jacket. When they were done there were more handshakes, and then the three who were leaving climbed on board. The doors were closed, and the engines changed pitch as the plane taxied towards the end of the skiway. They stood and watched. Thomas took more pictures, and Doc told him they would never capture the way things really were. Thomas said he'd give it a go all the same. The cold started creeping back. When Luke shuffled his feet for warmth he could hear the squeak of the snow beneath his boots. His ears were ringing from the lack of noise. From the end of the skiway the plane started moving towards them, picking up speed, the cliffs at that end of the shore a stark backdrop. For the first time Luke looked out across the Sound, the water still and grey and the far shore barely visible in the faint haze. The plane swept past them, and the pilot held her hand up to the window. They waved back, and watched the nose tip up into the air. The back of the plane seemed frozen to the ground for a moment and then it followed, climbing a few feet before lurching to the right and back to the left – 'Get up, you bugger, get up,' Doc was saying – and slumping back down to the snow. The noise was distant but they could hear the tone deepening as the plane slowed again, rolling towards the far end of the skiway.

Luke wasn't sure what had just happened. He couldn't see any smoke or flames. It was difficult to see, behind his sunglasses and beard, what Doc might be thinking.

They watched the plane turn a slow half-circle in the distance, and wait. Luke tried to catch Thomas's eye. There were banks of snow heaped up along the side of the skiway.

The plane started towards them again, gathering speed, a fine white spray thrown up on either side. The noise of it was thin against all the space around them. The front skis lifted, and again there was an awkward pause before the rear ski lifted as well. The wings lurched sharply to the left and the right – 'Oh shitting, shitting hell,' Doc said, his voice pitching higher – but this time the plane settled into a steady climb as it passed them, lifting away over the end of the skiway and heading towards the glacier at the far end of the Sound.

The silence started to settle.

'Right,' Doc said, lightly, as though the departure had been entirely standard. 'Let's get these stores up to the hut.' He fetched the skidoo and began loading crates onto the sleds that were tow-lined behind it. Luke watched the plane. It was small and red against the haze blowing up from the head of the glacier. It banked to the left, eking out a slow turn. It had the blown, flimsy look of a kite. It was still climbing as it passed them for the final time, out along the Sound towards the open sea and turning to follow the coastline north. Luke lost sight of it in the white glare.

Behind him, Doc was telling Thomas how to distribute the weight of the stores evenly across the sledges. He was raising his voice so that Luke would hear, which Luke took as a suggestion that he should be over there, helping. Subtext was the man's specialist subject, it was already clear.

'So, here we are,' Doc said, once Luke had joined them. 'Welcome to Station K. This is your first time here, I believe. I

42

myself have been previously, once or twice. Hell of a place. Quick reminder: I'm here as GTA—'

'GTA? General Territorial Administrator?'

'Obviously not. General Technical Assistant, as you know.'

'Technical General Assistant.'

'No, General Technical Assistant. GTA. It's not important.'

'Okay. GTA. Got it.'

'Good. Anyway, it's down to me to make sure everything runs smoothly and you can get your work done. I'm not in charge, obviously. But I do have a certain amount of experience and I would ask you to respect that. Fair?'

'Totally fair, Doc.'

'Team morale can be an issue in a remote field station like this, so it might be useful to run through a short debrief each evening, iron out any misunderstandings and so on. That okay with you?'

'You want to debrief us every evening?'

'Well, not formally, obviously. I just mean that we talk things over, straighten things out. It's not like I'm in charge.'

'But you'd like some debriefing to occur?'

'I think you're overcomplicating this.'

'I'm just trying to be clear, Doc.'

'Never mind. Let's get these stores stowed, and we can have smoko.'

He started the engine, and Luke told Thomas that he'd be keeping his briefs on in the evening, actually. They put their helmets on, and the two of them climbed onto the second skidoo and followed Doc. They headed across the flat ground and slowly up the slope towards the red field hut of Station K. Behind them, the sun on the water was metallic. Their progress was less dramatic than the word *skidoo* had led Luke to expect. The engine was loud and straining but they moved at a slow pace. It took twenty minutes to get to the hut, and three return trips to bring up all the supplies.

/

The hut made Luke think of the word *fjord*. There was something Scandinavian about it. Its walls were painted an iron-oxide red, and the roof was black corrugated iron. There was a veranda running along the front. It looked like a fisherman in a rugged sweater should come out, nod in their direction, and start working on his nets. As they stepped inside, Doc's shoulders dropped, and Luke watched him relax. He'd already told them about the history of the place; about the men who had built this place from scratch, landed by ship in a blizzard and living in tents while they raised the roof, and about the work Doc and his colleagues had done when they first arrived. It didn't look like much had changed since then. There were four bunks at the far end, with shelves and cubby-holes built in around them; a long table in the middle of the room, with benches on either side and the HF radio mounted above it; and a run of kitchen equipment along the near wall. There was an oil-fired stove that the last team had left running. On the wall there were maps and charts, newspaper cuttings, and photographs of previous residents. There was a bookcase, and a shelf of board games and jigsaw puzzles. It was several years since Doc had been back here, but he clearly still thought of the place as home. Some of the books on the shelves were his. There were pictures on the wall that he'd pinned up two decades before. The top bunk by the window had always been his, and he immediately swung himself up into it. 'Welcome to Station K., boys,' he said.

/

For the first two days they couldn't even go outside. The weather battered at the windows and they turned the stove up high. They talked about the schedule, and they drank a lot of tea. Thomas took a lot of pictures of the hut, and Doc asked him questions about lenses and file sizes. They kept their skeds with the radio operator at Bluff Point. Wind direction zero one zero. Windspeed two five knots. Present weather blowing snow, heavy.

On the third day they woke to silence and blue skies, and after breakfast they set out to clear the skiway. They had GPS reference work to get started on, but of course their first priority was to keep the station operational. Doc had a way of slipping these things out as if they didn't really need saying. As if he were agreeing with something they had already said. They went out to the storage shed, and Doc showed them how to hook up the groomers to the skidoos. They drove down the long bank from the field hut, rattling their way towards the black flags of the skiway with the groomers clattering behind them. The sky was clear and deeply blue. At the far end of the Sound the icebergs sat stately in the water, the light moving around them at odd angles. In the distance the silence was almost visible. On the back of the skidoo the noise was overwhelming.

They were at Station K. to update some of the mapping work that had been carried out along this stretch of the Peninsula for nearly four decades. Luke and Thomas were both post-doc researchers in Geographic Information Services, and skilled in the use and maintenance of GPS systems. Detailed mapping of the coastline had long since been completed, but the georeferencing they carried out here would address minor anomalies in the existing data. The word *anomaly* was used very deliberately. Doc had already told them he didn't like the word *mistake*. People do their best, he'd said. These are difficult circumstances.

They were also at Station K., as far as Luke could tell, to clean up all the shit that Doc and his colleagues had left behind over the last three decades. This, too, was couched in euphemism. *Rationalisation of storage systems* was talked about, and *localised restoration*. What that meant was clearing up the empty fuel barrels and testing the ground around them for contamination. It meant crating up the pieces of broken and abandoned machinery. It meant digging out the old rubbish tip and crating up the food tins, bottles, rags, and congealed magazines that were frozen in there.

And they were there to keep the skiway operational, which meant scraping it flat. *Flat* was an ambitious way of putting it; there were shallow ripples swirling across the packed snow, in patterns that described the eddying of wind across water, and it was impossible to scour all of them away. Their task was to break up the larger ridges with the groomer, working it across the frozen snow like a harrow. They worked backwards and forwards, a racket of iron and smashed ice dragging behind. The noise and vibration was wearing and the cold damp air crept into them. Luke and Thomas took it in turns to drive, and when he was sitting on the back Luke tried not to admit to himself that he was bored.

At break time the three of them gathered around Doc's skidoo and opened a manfood box. Thomas took a series of pictures, and kept looking at the back of the camera to see how they were turning out. There was a flask of coffee mixed with hot chocolate, and energy bars, and dried fruit. They sat on the skidoo seats in silence, their breath clouding above them. A light wind had picked up and the visibility was dropping.

'Doc?'

'Thomas.'

'Has anyone ever asked about calling this a *man*food box?'

'How's that?'

'I mean, you don't think it's problematic?'

'Well. It's just an old habit. It doesn't mean anything.'

'It means food for men, though, right?'

'No, it means food for people. Man as in *hu*-man.'

'But not man as in *wo*-man.'

'Oh, I see what you're getting at.'

'He's with you now, Thomas.'

'I think you're reading too much into it.'

'Do you?'

'I mean, we've actually had some excellent women working for the Institute, in more recent years. Some of them have even worked as GTAs.'

'Very modern.'

'You wouldn't know the difference, with some of them.'

'You wouldn't know the difference?'

'No, not at all. Honorary men, effectively.'

'Honorary, right. Got it.'

There was what Doc called *a drear mank* rolling in from the end of the Sound and settling through the valley, and the moisture soon started seeping into them. They packed away the manfood box and got back to work.

/

Twice a day they gathered for the scheduled radio communication with Main Base. The radio operator at Bluff Point cycled through every field station, asking for a brief report of the day's activities, weather readings, and any supply issues. Station K., time one eight zero zero, windspeed one five knots, contrast poor, present weather nil, no injuries or immediate concerns. The tone was brisk, but beneath the reporting the message was still essentially: hello, we're here, we're alive. Take care. Sleep tight. Copy that. Out. The importance of the schedules had been emphasised in training. Any failure to respond to the daily skeds would trigger an emergency response. Silence was a call for help, in this context. Each evening, as they listened to the other stations checking in and waited their turn, Thomas liked to track their locations around the map of the Peninsula; each response like the brief puff of smoke from a distant flare.

/

'I packed my kitbag, and in it I put: an axe.'

Luke turned from the sink at one end of the hut and caught Thomas's eye.

'Really, Doc?'

'Come on, Luke,' Doc said, from the easy chair by the stove. 'Your turn. No shirkers.'

'Shirkers, now?'

'Let me tell you something, Luke. There's no television here, no radio—'

'Yeah, it's peaceful. Right?'

'It's definitely peaceful,' Thomas said, from his laptop.

'Yes, but you'll find the quietness gets a bit much after a while. I've found, over the years, that a little structured recreation helps keep the time passing, and keeps a team together.'

'Okay. I might just finish these pots first though.'

'It's not as if you can go anywhere else for entertainment, now.'

'True, Doc.'

'The nearest humans are about three hundred miles away. And they're Russian.'

'Got it.'

'And you'd probably die on the way.'

'Cheerful.'

'So: I packed my kitbag and in it I put … an axe. Luke?'

'Yeah, after the pots. Thomas, you take my go.'

'I packed my kitbag,' Thomas said, 'and in it I put: an axe, and a belay.'

'Belay, good. I packed my kitbag and in it I put an axe, a belay, and a crampon.'

/

When the weather was clear they trekked out from the field hut to take GPS readings. They loaded more equipment than they needed, and carried food and shelter in case they were caught out and needed to lay up in the field. The prepping and loading of supplies took a long time. They asked Doc's advice when they needed it, but he made a point of waiting to be asked. I'm only here to assist, he told them. Generally. Technically. They chose unambiguous reference points for their readings: a VHF repeater unit that had been installed thirty years ago, and featured in successive aerial photographs; the junction of two ridges at the base of the K7 mountain; a narrow slab of rock at the very end of Garrard Ridge. They travelled by skidoo as far as possible, hauling the equipment on foot when the ground became too steep.

When they got to the reference point they worked efficiently, setting up the tripods and the GPS base units, running through the boot sequence and taking each reading more than once. Each reading took an hour to record, as the unit tracked several satellites through the sky and calibrated the position to an accuracy of a few centimetres. Doc brewed hot chocolate while they waited, and told them stories about his early years at Station K.

The evenings were long and still. The sun didn't set, but only dipped weakly towards the horizon before climbing again into the sky. The water in the bay was flat and dark and the silence was vast. There was work to be done but there were also these long stretches of waiting. They ate a lot of food and they scrubbed the pots and dishes and table and floor. They read the books Doc had collected over the years, which were almost all about Antarctica. Thomas edited his photos. They wrote up their field notes from the day, and kept their skeds with Bluff Point, and cleaned their kit again, and still there were hours of the evening to spare.

The night-time was no such thing. The continent kept its face towards the sun and the ice slowly softened. The mountains climbed sharply away from the valley and the glaciers tongued down towards the sea. In the crevasses that ran across the lower mountain slopes the light fell bluely down, dimming towards the depths.

A light breeze blew dustings of ice and snow further up the slopes.

Radio signals passed very occasionally through the air.

/

'I packed my kitbag and in it I put an axe, a belay, a crampon, a drybag, an egg, a flashgun, a gold bar, a harness, and an ice pick.'

'How long have you been doing this, Doc?'

'Sorry, what, this game?'

'Yeah, this game. No, how long have you been working here?'

'Thomas, it's your turn. This is my thirty-third season on the Peninsula, Luke.'

'Thirty-three? Jesus. Have you never got bored?'

'Bored? Have you looked outside? Who would get bored of that?'

'Yeah, it's great, I know.'

'Obviously.'

'Obviously. But after a while I mean. Don't you kind of get the hang of it?'

'The *hang* of it?'

'I'm just saying, isn't there a limit to how many icebergs you can look at, or mountains you can climb?'

'You realise Antarctica is a big place, I take it.'

'Right. But most of it you don't go to. Most of the time you've worked here you've been driving skidoos, moving fuel drums, putting up tents, flying up and down this stretch of the Peninsula. And you've been a General Technical Assistant that whole time, right?'

'They used to call us Field Hands, actually.'

'Field Hands?'

'Quite.'

'GTA sounds better than Field Hand, Doc.'

'I'd prefer Expedition Guide myself.'

'Assistant Technician?' Thomas suggested, from behind his laptop.

'Don't get me wrong, Doc. This is amazing. I'm never going to be able to explain to people back home how amazing this is. I just don't know if it would carry on being amazing for that long. Like, how amazed can one man be?'

'Ass Tech, for short?' Thomas said.

'Whizzywig, Luke.'

'Come again?'

'Whizzywig. What you see is what you get. I know this place. I've worked all across the Peninsula. I know my way around. It's a timeless landscape. Nothing changes. Thomas, it's still your turn.'

'I packed my kitbag and in it I put an axe—'

'When I'm back in Cambridge, things are always changing: new roads, new estates, buildings knocked down and thrown up. Litter everywhere. Tourists crowding the pavements.'

'—a belay, a crampon, a drybag, an—'

'Here, there's no one messing with the place. If there's any litter, it's because we dropped it. And we damn well pick it up again.'

'—a harness, an ice pick, and a jerrycan.'

'If I climb up Garrard Ridge and find a patch of yellow snow, it'll be because I took a piss there last week. Pardon my French.'

'Class.'

'It's not anyone else's.'

'You know we have a toilet block now, Doc?'

'There's a purity about being here, you see? Or, well, not purity; simplicity. It's difficult to explain.'

'No, you're doing a great job there, Doc.'

'I think it's fair to say I feel more at home here than I do at home.'

'Really?'

'Yes, really. It's your turn, Luke.'

'Right. Okay. Axe, belay, crampon, drybag, whatever whatever, jerrycan, kitbag.'

'You married, Doc?'

'Yes, Thomas, I am. Two children. Left home now.'

'How's your wife with you being down here so much?'

'We have an understanding.'

'Understanding, okay. Wait, Luke, you can't put a kitbag in a kitbag.'

'I just did.'

'Doc?'

'Sounds valid to me.'

'Doc, have you told your wife you feel more at home down here?'

'Not in so many words, Luke, no. And your family?'

'What about them?'

'How do they feel about you coming down here?'

'Yeah, my mum was nervous about it.'

'It's your go, Doc.'

'I packed my kitbag and in it I put the following: axe, belay, crampon, drybag, egg, flashgun, gold bar, harness, ice pick, jerry-can, kitbag, and a lemon.'

'A lemon? No way, Doc. There are no lemons down here.'

'Where are your family from anyway, Luke?'

'My family? London. New Cross.'

'No, but—'

'Don't go there, Doc.'

'Go where, Thomas? I'm just asking.'

'Doc.'

'Where are they from originally though?'

'Originally, Doc?'

'Yes. I'm just curious.'

'You're curious.'

'I didn't mean anything by it.'

'No, it's fine. They're from Norway.'

'Norway?'

'You sound surprised. Yeah. They're from Tromsø, in the far north of Norway. It's why I'm so well suited to these conditions. Like, temperamentally.'

/

The silence rolled down from the ridges and across the valley and seeped in through the insulated doors, settling over the bunks and shelves and table like a fine dust as the three of them cleared away the mugs and got ready for bed. They lowered the blackout blinds, and a semblance of dusk came into the room. It wasn't enough to ease the crystalline alertness each of them felt, and the bunks creaked as they took turns to move around and settle and look for a new position that might lull them closer to sleep.

/

They groomed the snow on the skiway again. *Flat* was still an exaggeration. The air was sharp in their lungs but they warmed up quickly. There was a problem with one of the groomers, and Doc worked on it with Thomas while Luke got a brew on. *Groomer* seemed like a gentle word for something that was basically all iron and spikes. When they broke for drinks Doc mentioned again that he'd painted the orange fuel drums along the skiway himself, working with Planky Carruthers. He had told Luke and Thomas about this already. He had told them several detailed stories about his early seasons at Station K. The field hut had been built years earlier, but Doc and his colleagues had been responsible for expanding the station, building the new storage sheds, the waste facilities, and the incinerating toilets. Doc had become rather fond of the place by the time they'd finished, he said.

When they had gone over the whole skiway they parked up for another break, and Doc said he wanted to do a final inspection run. There was a flight coming in for refuelling and he wanted to be confident of the conditions. They sat on the skidoo while he drove to the end of the skiway and back several times. His inspection was very thorough. Whirls of snow began to flurry around them. The wind picked up and the flurries sharpened. By the time Doc was at the far end of the skiway they could no longer see him, and for a while there was silence before he appeared. The weather thickened quickly, and each time he drove away it took him longer to come back into view. The headlights of the skidoo cut butterishly through the murk, and although Thomas and Luke said nothing, they were both unnerved by the silence before he returned each time.

'Can you imagine, though?'

'Don't even say it.'

'If he just never came back?'

'What did I just say?'

'Seriously, though. What would we do?'

'Simple. Straight back to the hut, get on the radio, wait for the weather to clear.'

'Don't panic?'

'Don't fucking panic. Correctamundo.'

'Which way's the hut, Luke?'

'Fuck off.'

'Seriously though, which way is it now?'

'That way. Up there.'

'I don't know if it is. That might be the way to the glacier.'

'No way.'

'Or the sea.'

'Yeah, stop it now.'

'We could set off back to the hut and just – sploosh.'

'*Sploosh?*'

'Sploosh. One wrong step – sploosh.'

'It's definitely that way.'

'How long do you think you'd survive in the water?'

'Cut it out now.'

'Five minutes? Two minutes?'

'So we'd sit tight until the weather cleared.'

'Sploosh.'

'Seriously, Thomas.'

'You'd go into shock, I reckon.'

'Come on, man. We've got GPS, we've got compasses.'

'Look at the GPS. Which way is it? That way?'

'It's definitely that way. Hang on, it's refreshing.'

'Got it? That way?'

'Hang on. Shit. Shit. Okay. It's not exactly that way. Shit.'

'Sploosh.'

'Yeah, sploosh.'

They crouched behind the skidoo, bracing themselves against the wet wind, waiting for Doc to return. The snow was near horizontal now, building up in layers against the folds and ridges of their jackets. The noise of the wind was building. They waited for Doc to return.

/

'*Station K., Station K., this is Bluff Point, Bluff Point, come in, over.*'

'Bluff Point this is Station K., Station K., receiving.'

'*Station K., confirm status update, over.*'

57

'All personnel accounted for. No injuries or immediate concerns. Programme running to schedule. Over.'

'*That's good to hear, Doc. New boys still not causing any trouble?*'

'Wind direction two seven zero degrees, windspeed ten knots, visibility ten kilometres, contrast moderate, temperature minus three, present weather nil, over.'

'*Received. Thanks, Doc. Good talking to you as always. Out.*'

/

In the evening from the top of Garrard Ridge Luke and Thomas looked down towards the field hut of Station K. The sky was clear and the sun was high. *Evening* was barely the right word, despite it being close to midnight. A thin line of soft grey smoke climbed from the hut's metal stove pipe. Thomas mounted the GPS unit on its tripod and waited for the boot sequence to complete. On the far side of the bay the mountains reared up into the sky. They could see Doc pacing distantly between the hut and the stores. From here it was unclear what he was doing; he approached the stacks of oil-drums, paused, and walked back to the hut, and then he did the same with the storage shed, the tool shed, the covered waste depot, and the skidoos.

'I think he's just counting things again.'

'Man loves to count.'

The GPS unit beeped its calibration confirmations, and they uploaded the figures.

/

The field hut swayed and shuddered on its footings, the heavy canvas straps straining to hold it down. The smoke from the chimney and the yellow light spilling from the small windows gave it the look of a pilot vessel making its way through a storm. Inside, the timber panelling creaked and the oil-fired stove roared. There was condensation on the glass. Visibility ten metres. Present weather heavy blowing snow. The kettle whistled once again and Doc poured milky sweet tea by the pint.

/

'Doc, can I ask you a question?'

'Shoot from the hip, Luke.'

'Shoot from the; right. Okay. Where does *Doc* come from?'

'Ah. Well, I'm certainly not a medical doctor.'

'No.'

'It's just one of those things, I suppose. It started somewhere along the line, and it just stuck.'

'You don't remember where it came from?'

'Not really, no.'

'Okay. Cool story. Thanks for sharing.'

/

The iron-blood paintwork of Station K. was a distant smudge on the ice and getting smaller. The bodies breathing inside made a faint yellow fog of the windows. The bodies came, and they went. Their traces softened the ice a little further each year. The ice slipped and broke into the water. The icebergs turned, and decayed, and traced the eddying currents of the bay towards the wild open reaches of the sea. The daylight was silence. The bodies breathed in their narrow wooden shelter. The weather closed in again. The bodies spilled out from their shelter and scattered slowly across the snow. They carried packs and poles and radios. They moved further apart. The long dusk was coming, and afterwards the night would press down for months. There was movement in the water, and the sky darkened above the glacier. A weather system moved in from the ridge.

/

Luke was the first out of bed in the morning, as he had been since they'd arrived; the first one out of the door and down to the toilet shed. Being an early riser had its rewards. He closed the door gently behind him and followed the path away down the scree slope to the north, past the stacks of oil-drums and cases of supplies, the pallets and tat that had accumulated over the years. The path to the toilet shed was marked by flags and tapes in case of bad weather. There was no bad weather today. It was another fine morning at Station K.

When he was up this early he liked to leave the toilet door wide open. The view was unreal, when the weather was clear. The deep blue sky and the sharp white edges of the mountains. Icebergs turning slowly in the Sound. They'd been here three weeks now and he still wasn't used to it. He didn't know how he would tell people about it when he got home. There weren't the words. He looked up towards the head of the Sound, to the snow blowing across the top of the glacier. The mountain ranges beyond the glacier were more than fifty miles away. There was nobody between him and them. There was nobody for a few hundred miles beyond that. He'd never been this far from other people. He never would be again.

There was a crunching of footsteps, and his view of the mountain was blocked suddenly by Thomas, leaning on the doorframe and heaving for breath.

'You know why they put doors on toilet blocks, Luke?'

'No, mate, why's that?'

'So I don't have to look at your junk while I'm waiting my turn.'

'No one's asking you to look, mate. Just back up to the hut until you see the vacant sign.'

'What vacant sign? Is this something you've not told us about?'

'Metaphorically. If I'm not in the hut where else am I going to be? Keep your eyes up.'

'If you're embarrassed you should have shut the door.'

'I've got nothing to be embarrassed about. Is Doc up yet? Anyway, fuck off and let me finish.'

'The Doc's still snoring. Sleeping it off. Anyway, don't mind me, mate. Go ahead and finish. I can wait.'

'Fuck off now.'

'Fuck this far off?'

'Like, fuck right around the corner off. All the way off.'

He watched Thomas go, and pulled the door shut. Even with the light on it was suddenly very dark. He finished what he was doing and headed back up to the hut.

After breakfast and the morning sked they talked about plans for the day. They had completed their mapping schedule with three days spare, and Thomas was keen to do some photography around the shore of the Sound. Doc insisted again that photographs would never capture what they could see down here, but he had several suggestions for locations to shoot from. There were some maintenance tasks he wanted a hand with first, but after lunch they loaded Thomas's camera bags and tripods onto the skidoo with a manfood box, and headed down across the skiway towards the Sound.

There was a broad rim of first-year ice around the shore, and Thomas spent some time with the play of the light from the water against it. He had Doc and Luke both posing for portraits.

'You'll be putting this on your *Instagram*, I suppose?' Doc asked.

'I mean, maybe. Mostly I'm hoping to put an exhibition together, but I might post some of these, yeah. Is that all right?'

'Doesn't bother me. I don't look at that kind of thing. If it helps you get more favourites, it's fine by me.'

'Yeah. Favourites. Okay.'

'Doc, maybe you should work it a bit more?'

'Okay, Luke. I think we're done now, are we?'

Thomas was setting up a long lens, and looking over towards the cliffs of Priestley Head with a frustrated expression.

'Is there a problem, Thomas?'

'I don't know, Doc. It just needs something to give it a bit of perspective, you know?'

9 /

Doc Wright crashed into the storm porch and forced the door shut. For a moment it still hurt to breathe. He rubbed the numb rawness from his face. The back of his head was still throbbing, but there was no bruising or blood and he wasn't sure now that anything had struck him at all. He peeled off his waterproofs, his fingers fumbling fatly with the zips. He held the coat hooks for support. He didn't know how long he had been down. Couldn't recall getting on the skidoo and pointing it up to the plateau. Some kind of muscle memory. Found himself halfway back with the engine roaring before he'd quite got himself together. The storm was nailing itself to the door. He could hear the radio in the main room. *Come in, Doc, come in.* He thought the two lads would have been here by now. The pain in his head was coming and going. When it went there was a numbness. His breathing was still ragged. He heard someone on the radio, asking him to respond. Luke. He heard Luke on the radio. He hung up his wet gear. Slowly. He was working slowly. The meltwater puddled on the floor. He sat on the locker to ease off his boots. There was pain but it didn't quite register. There was a problem with his right foot. There was a problem with his whole right leg. Luke was still trying him on the radio. The sound of the storm softened as a drift built back up against the door. He numbed at the rubness of his face. He moved through to the main room and went straight to the desk. The air was still. The air was still and warm and he let his weight sail into the chair. Luke was on the radio, asking Thomas to confirm his location. There was not yet a response. Each time he called there was a gap and then a rush of white noise like applause. *Doc, come in. Doc? Do you read me, Doc?* Between transmissions the silence was heavy. The storm had settled to a white-out now. It was something almost like a fog. It was like a blanket thrown over the hut. It would lift soon enough. It was likely Thomas was just staying put until conditions improved. He was a sensible lad. He hoped Luke was doing the same. Where were they? He poured a drink. He reached the first aid kit down from the shelf and attended to his injury. When he peeled the sock from his foot there was nothing wrong. He thought he would find a blister or worse but there was nothing. There were lights flashing on the radio but there was no sound. He emptied his glass. He eased himself to his feet. He rawed the rum nubness of his face. No. Rubbed. Rubbed the rum rawness. No. Radio. *Doc, Thomas, come in. Come in, Doc? Thomas? Fuck's sake, anyone?* There was no call for the language. He looked out into the white darkness and listened to Luke trying to raise Thomas on the radio. He looked at the radio. There was something he needed to do. He crossed the floor of the hut to the window. It was a long way. Everything leaned over to the right. The floor rose and fell. The glass was cold against his face. The weather was solid. They were good lads but this was their first season South. They didn't yet have that indistinct. The cold was glass against his face. It was not unpleasant. He leaned into it. He waited. The buck stopped with him and he was used to that. But they damn well needed a sense of personal responsibility and they weren't always ready. They'd always had someone else looking out for them: parents or team leaders or expensive insurance policies. Down here, you either got yourself out of trouble or you stayed in it. He'd known men crawl the length of a glacier with a broken leg, in his time. And he'd known men stay put. They made their choices. They left Doc to talk to the wives, months later, at the memorial services. He talked of you often, Bridget. He died doing what he loved best. Try to remember that. He was a hero until the end. The weight on his foot was worse now. There was glass. His numb rubbed the cold of his face. No. The radio. The radio. White noise breaking in like apple sauce. Applause. Thomas was on the radio. The light through the hut window brightened. The storm would be rolling out again. Visibility lifting out again. The ridge and the ridge beyond that and the steam of mown snow against the sky. Snow blowers. Mowers. Blown snow. Luke on the radio asking Thomas to confirm his location. How many years he'd been coming here now. All that experience had to count for something. Everything he'd learned when he first came down. Working with the men who had built this place. Mowbray, and Maggs. The two of them telling him and Carruthers the stories. Navy boys brought us down with supplies. Took a month to get here. He and Planky Carruthers in their first season, both of them a little disappointed by the way things worked. A whole lot of safety protocols and not much room for adventure. Would say he'd bonded with Planky on the subject. He'd seen Planky around in Cambridge over the years, of course.

They'd been at different colleges but they moved in the same circles. The man's name was known. Their girls had been friends, it turned out. One night in the mess Planky had called him *Doc*, and the name stuck. Seemed as good a name as any. There was no reason or rhyme. Mowbray and Maggs brought them down to Station K. to work on some maintenance. Talking about their first sight of the place. When they'd entered the Sound the commanding officer asked Mowbray up to the bridge to take stock. Would have been a glorious sight. Tall mountain peaks on either side of the Sound, stark white against the grey skies, set back behind a system of ridges and crevasses that stepped down to the shore. Glacier at the head of the valley, moving inexorably towards the sea. None of it surveyed, or mapped in detail. None of it named. When they landed supplies they would have been setting foot on virgin territory. Half a dozen of them left at the edge of the fast-ice, watching the navy ship leave the bay. Left to their own devices. Sink or swim. Camping out on the plateau for a month, hauling up materials for the field hut. Team of dogs to help with the hauling. Malcolm Maggs was the best chippy the Institute ever had, the way Mowbray told it. Man was a magician with wood. A running joke about getting the work done by nightfall. Lay up in the tent until the weather breaks, lads. Keep the dogs tethered. Nightfall was three months away. I said Maggs, if you're whittling another flute, I will stick it where the sun don't shine. Days until the weather broke. By the time Doc heard the story it was already twenty years old. Sometimes he felt like he'd arrived in Antarctica a generation too late. All the real work had already been done. Thomas was on the radio, giving out coordinates. The coordinates were confusing. Doc tried to picture

66

them on the map. Thomas radioed a correction. Luke was saying something else. He was shouting. Doc could bring every square of the map to mind. The first drafts of it had been made at that chart table right there, years before his time. There were photos of the first surveyors, ice on their goggles, up on the ridges with theodolites. All different now. Brew stop and smoko. Weather mank and miserly. The radio again. Luke on the radio. The words tumbling jumbled out. He turned from the window and the raw froze and ell. Floor flows and fell. Rose and fell. Thirty years with the Institute, Anna. Has it been that long? Did you miss me? Thirty years and only one season he didn't make it down to the ice. There's no great pride to be had in that, sweetheart. Not a proud man. These are just the simple facts. It's a long time to be gone. Too long for some. It's a commitment. You need the commitment. The job keeps you away from the family longer than might be preferred. But you understand this is part of the work. There are sacrifices to make and we have to be prepared to make them. Couldn't make the cut. Didn't last long. Down for a season or two and then back to civilian life. No better than tourists. Waiting to see how these two worked out. They were passing muster so far. Anna, these lads are okay. Sleeping in the bunks Maggs had built all those years ago. Cubby-holes for books and journals, and folding wooden shutters for privacy. Not much privacy to be had when they were sleeping and eating and working in the one room, but that was just something they had to get used to. Not everyone had managed that, over the years. It was part of the weeding-out process. Anna, I'm worried about these two. His face was glass against the cold. There was a pain in his head. The floor was a long way away. There were voices on the

67

radio again. Thomas. Luke. They weren't making sense. Most General Techs moved on to something else after a few years but he and Planky had kept coming back. Something addictive about it. Every year a different area of operations. Honing their skills. Getting to know the territory better and better. Kept finding an excuse to get back to Station K. Something special about the place. Always a small team. Private. When he'd done twenty years they gave him a bauble for the mantelpiece. A small drinks reception at Cambridge HQ. Anna, were you proud of me then? Are you proud of me now? Will that be enough for you, Robert? Do you still need to go every year? Sometimes the wives won't understand. Join me in a toast. Tinkling glasses. Small, quiet applause. Anna putting her drink down and leaving the room. Hardly think this is reasonable now. These are the sacrifices we make, lads. Not everyone will understand. Thomas's voice on the radio. White noise. Interference. Luke's voice. Transmission over. Transmission recommenced. Thomas again. White noise. He stared at the radio. Through the window the world was white and wild. Through the window a figure loomed into view, faint and muddled, the red jacket raw against the weather. Luke on the radio asking Thomas to repeat. A storm of white noise and the transmission was broken. *Location is. Sheet. Adrift. Heading landfall at Priestley. Confirm. Adrift.* Doc watched through the window the figure coming towards him. It was Luke. So he hadn't remained in place either. The discipline was shot. He could picture in the distance the line of mountains beyond the far shore of the Sound. But from here he couldn't see the water, the ice, the skiway. He couldn't see the flags of the storage sheds two hundred yards away. Couldn't see Thomas. Luke was rattling against the door. Trying to clear the snow. Thomas's voice again. *Luke? Luke? Did you get that? Are you there? Come in, come in?* Wright turned away from the window, heading for the radio and the map. Anna was required. Action. He was the assistant. General. The technical general assistant. He was required to assist. He was required to take action. He had the experience required. He moved towards the radio. He went over on his weak right foot and hit the floor hard. He floored the numb faceness of his raw No. Rawed the rub. The rum. The nub. The light dimmed and brightened and dimmed again dim. White noise like a pause. The radio rattled raw.

And, and, and. Up again, up again. Stand. Christ but what now. The pain in his head and the weakness. His weak right side. Numb the face rub. What was wrong. What was up. What's up, Doc? Planky's first greeting. First joke. He had never understood the joke. It was a slight of some kind. Planky's repartee was the sort that tended to only flow downhill. But no matter. Was as good a name as any. Not the easiest of men to get on with. He had his abrasive side. But a bloody good general technician. Attention to detail was second to none. One of the best techs the Institute had known. Was a shame, what had happened. Was the chance they all took, coming down here. Obviously. Was always understood. *Confirm. Adrift. Request update. Over.* Thomas's voice on the radio. The radio rattled raw. Invoke the protocol. The Institute has an emergency protocol. Handled a few just such situations himself. Handled just such a few. Handled a situation as such. The light dim dimmed and the brightly raw. Accurate confirmation of the location and condition. Status updates.

69

Situation upstate. This no such emergency now yet though of course. No need to concern Base Command. No now. Up, up, up. At the chart table and studied. Studied the map and plot Thomas's course. Harked up the locations Thomas reported and protract the line of project. The heading fared seemly constant. The same wind that had sought the splash in was storming Thomas's ice floe correctly along. The necessary man of action was clear. Plan. Necessarily plan. Of axes. What now the words Christ now. At the funeral Anna talking to Planky's wife for a very long time. Something in it that Doc didn't understand. They both looked as upset as each other. In the days afterwards Anna barely spoke. He had done everything he could, he told her. These things happened when you went South. Okay, she said. I'm always careful, he told her; you know that. Okay, she said, again. When Planky fell through, the dogs had gone with him. Their whining the first sign of something wrong. Out on a recreational trip from Bluff Point. Doc on the lead sledge, Planky on the second. Ten dogs apiece. The area well mapped. Route avoiding known crevasses. The unknown unknowns. Dogs all essentially retired. Institute had stopped working them seriously years before. Men like Mowbray and Maggs were still very attached. Kept them trained up for recreational runs. Planky and Doc had earned a week's break and planned their trip carefully. The lead sledge must have weakened the frozen snow bridging the crevasse. Planky's dogs got across and then his sledge went through. Thing they all dreaded. Stories of near misses and slow rescues. Would barely register what was happening before you were down in the cold blue light. The crevasse was narrow. The sledge didn't plummet through open space but scraped and slipped all the way

70

down. Dogs started whining when they were dragged backwards by the traces into the hole. Scratching at the ice, unable to get a foothold, snapping at each other in confused fury. All happened slowly but not slowly enough. Doc running back to cut the lines. Slow slow too slow. Longest trace thirty feet. Lead dog came to a halt on the edge of the crevasse, the sledge wedged somewhere below. Dog's name was Sandy. Sat and licked her front paws clean, as though nothing was wrong. She was generally given the lead trace because she was of such an even temperament. The other dogs feared her. Doc was somewhat fond. Always first at the feeding bowls, but she made sure the others got their share. She was rather a matronly figure. Just before he got to her, ready to cut the trace, there was a commotion from the dogs in the crevasse, and Sandy was jerked back and over the edge. She didn't even have time to look surprised. Make contact now, make radio contact. Thomas, Thomas, this is Doc, do you hear me. Stand by for a brief quickening. Situation upstate. Over. Over. Listen and no words come. Listen and the cold like glass. Listen and the distant white noise like apple sauce. So wait now. Rest now. Of course. Perhaps he had been more cavalier in the early years, before they'd had children. Children change you in that way. They give you a reason to stick around. When he'd mentioned this she'd asked if she wasn't reason enough. Of course, but that's different, he said. You know what I mean. Both children, each year when he'd come back from the south, had treated him like a stranger. Wouldn't be picked up, wouldn't be held, screamed when Anna left the room. It's only to be expected, she said. Perhaps if you shaved your beard? She was given to these non sequiturs. It was difficult sometimes to make the adjustment.

They all felt it. After months on the ice, living elementally, thinking only of work and best practice, eating for calories, pumping fuel, cleaning stores, tracking progress through the work schedules, no distractions, no unwanted noises, no persons unknown. After that, coming home was a shock to the system. Everything so dirty and chaotic. Cluttered. People everywhere wandering aimlessly around. And in recent years, people glued to the light of their phones. Light addicts. It made a man miss the simplicity of life down South. The purity of it. The clarity. You were never there anyway, how would you know? Frank, the older child. Or it could have been Sara. Both of them threw versions of this at him at one time or another. When the boy had been rude to his mother. As a young adult. And been reminded of how much he owed her. How much had been sacrificed in his upbringing. You were never there anyway. How would you know? Light addicts. Walking around shining the lights in their eyes. Everything was for your sake. The work being done down there. She understood. They all understood. Deep down. No glory in the work of a general tech but the work wouldn't happen without them. All that science, the oceanography, the atmospheric stuff, hole in the bloody ozone layer. Five years, it had taken those men in the photographs to carry out the survey of Station K. On foot. With theodolites. Drawing up the results by hand, overlaying with the air photographs. Aerial. Thomas and his bloody corrections. Can we just say anomaly. Mistake is a bit loaded. No problem, Doc. Sorry. Yes. Christ. Anomalies. *Thomas, come in. This is Luke, Luke. Thomas are you fucking there? Doc? Over.* Between radio transmissions the roar of the wind was a kind of silence. The installation had this effect. Isolation. Insulation. It was like a blanket flown over the hut. It would lift soon enough. It was likely Thomas had just put the radio down, and was conserving the batteries improved. Luke should be doing the same. Where was Luke now. Luke was outside now. *Hello, come in, this is Thomas, over?* The light in the hut was murky and the shadows were everywhere. His head felt wrong. There was no pain but a weakness. The feeling came and went. There were lights flashing on the radio but there was no sound. He poured a drink and emptied his glass. He rawed the rum nubness of his face. No. Rubbed. Rubbed the rum rawness. No. Radio. Something was rattling against the door. The light brightened and he went to the window. There was something he should. Something was wrong. Anna, by the beside of him. Her long dark hair pinned back on her head. Always that surprise of her. Hello, it's you. Hello, of course, it's you again. In the morning. There you are. At the airport. Hello again. This is not a love story. But here we still are, of course. Of course. Her eyes, hello, the surprise of her. Late nights in the kitchen working hours on her own work, lost in some calculation, while he found a radio or a computer or some other widget to repair. And up. And look, up, it's you, of course, again, the surprise. Rest now. Come here now, will you. The hard wooden floor soften. Come now. Anna, wait. No more. One more. Something wrong. Some work to be done. Some will to be done. Anna, wait. The surprise of her. Later what she said. At the funeral. The coffin. The three days it took to recover Planky's body. Wedged beneath an overhang in the ice, two hundred feet down. Had wanted to climb down and get to him, while there was still a chance. But was instructed to wait. Safe rope procedure. Chain of command. They had to wait for a support team to arrive. There was some challenging ropework involved. They got him out just before a storm blew in. The main runway was closed for a week. They had to keep him in the cold store while they waited for a flight. At the funeral Anna telling him she knew this was what he wanted. What did she mean, he'd asked her; what was it he wanted? All this. White lilies in vases, varnished coffin, colleagues in funeral black, lonely widow stooping low. The heroic death. For God's sake look after my people. All that. The organ playing, and the sunlight streaming through the high chapel windows. I'd prefer to be buried down South, he told her. It was a joke but it went unappreciated. Something still. Wrong. Get up, get up off the floor. Stand.

The field hut at Station K. had been built with an integrated boot-room entrance, to allow for the removal of wet-weather gear and the exclusion of cold air on entry and exit so the boot room the storm door and so on. Heard Luke kick away the snow that had drifted up against the door and push his way in. He called through and asked if Luke had any immediates or injurious concerns. There was a pause. Doc? You okay? Infirmative. What. Affirmative. He waved an arm towards Luke to warn him off coming into the room with his weather gear on. The boy should know better than that. Luke stepped back into the boot room, but held the door open. What have they said at Main Base? He didn't respond immediately; he concentrated on plotting the projected path along the Sound. Doc? What have they said? What's the plan? He stood and gestured at the maps. There was no need to concern Bluff Point with this. The activity had been ill-advised. Was best remedied solo, soon. Plan the plan here. He showed Luke the projected route, indicating the wind direction. We trek among to the Head, the Priest, here, and back around, behind, the normal-east side to averagely – here – and landfall we, re, we, re claim we cover. Luke was looking at him. With a something expression. Instubborn. Subordinate. That type of language was discouraged these days. You sure you're okay, Doc? Rubbed his face. It was sure where he'd fallen. Sore. He was sure. Shore lips, he said. Sore lips, I'm sure. He laughed. Luke nodded. The standard personal radio handsets issued by the Antarctic Research Institute had been selected for robustness in the field and for reliable battery life at sub-zero temperatures. Battery life remained a key concern and the main. *This is Thomas, come in, this is Thomas, over.* Copy that, this am Dire, Doctor, Wire. Wright. Stand by for a brief quickening. Over. *Repeat that, please? Over.* Situation upstate. Standby. Over. He pain in his head and he lean over. Plan here. Trek around the Head and here. Have you run the plan past Base Commander? Luke query, question. Are they sending support? Aerial support? He shook his head and folding maps. This remains an in team, he said. Quiet. In team sit rep. Station. He sat and the colour fall. Music. What.

Stand by, Thomas, stand by. Pause. Rush of white noise. Luke watching. Thomas, Thomas, do you copy? More white noise. Like apples. Applause. *Copy [...]* Stand by for a brief quickening. Quick briefing. Situation upstate. He rubbed his jaw. The sore muscles were twisting his words. He shook his head. *Standing by, Doc, over.* He passed the radio to Luke, shaking his head again. Thomas, this is Luke, over. *Go ahead, over.* Listen, we've calculated your landing zone and will travel over land to meet you

75

there. Use the emergency flare to mark your landing spot, when you land. Over. [...] *serious* [...] *aerial support?* [...] Broken transmission, please repeat, over. Tell him to conserve the banteries. Pantries. Batteries. Tell him to conserve the batteries. *Repeat, is this a serious plan? Are* [...] *you* [...] *they sending aerial support? Luke? Seriously? Over.* Confirm, that's the plan. Recommended you conserve battery life on the radio, use the emergency flares, over. *Mate? Are they sending aerial support?* Tell him, he said. He paused. He could feel Luke watching him, waiting. He knew what the boy was thinking. But he'd only had that one drink. Two. He'd fallen. His face. He wasn't as young as he'd once been. Tell him this remains and in team stitching. This restrains a steam train in the station. He looked at Luke. His face was raw. He rummed the nub rawness. He nodded. What.

The field hut at Station K. was constructed in 1965 and with storage facility accessed careful storage. Loading supply sled for the risk assessment. Rescue. Assessment. Check. First aid supplies, check, ropes, check, rescue sack, manfood boxes, pup tent, check, spare radio, batteries, fuel, check, flares, check. Work quickly. Luke asking question question question. What if the wind shifts, Doc? What if the visibility? When will the fuel? Adrenalin in the boy's voice. No help. Keep control. Keep active. No need for help. No need for Main Base. Doc we should tell Main Base. Christ obviously, of course. Secure load and checks. Here. Radio I radio now. Secure load. Luke busy with loading skidoo. Wait here I radio now. Now back inside the hut. Quiet quiet still. Sit. Quiet. Radio. Lights. Radio. There was something he needed to do. Situation un control. Stand by for a brief quickening. Quick briefing. Situation upstate. Rub jaw. Sore muscles. Twist words. Shake head. Long wait. Words stuck. Okay. No problem. Radio silent and lights. No need to concern. Something he needed to. Outside in weather Luke ready. Fall. Fell. Sore lips. Numb faith. Look, Luke. Face raw. Rum the nub rawness. The kit was ready. Skidoo was running and final checks of course. Doc did they say. Doc what did they say at Main Base. Yes, yes, of course, of course. Situation in hand. Weather wild blast. No weather to drive into. Situation must. Soon will we around the landing zone. Check straps and kit and tow lines fuel. Luke too close. Standing. Luke shouting slow. Why shout. Do – you – want – me – to – drive? Why. Of course. Why Luke was asking a thing. He leaned towards a reply and found. Felt. Felt himself losing balance. Why. What. Lean. Fall. Up now, stand.

Team of dogs pulling a sled at full tilt one of the most glorious experiences of life in the field. Experience by very few. Sight of a dozen well-fed dogs packed with muscle with joy surging forward. The slashing of the sled runners across the ice. And the silence over everything, of course. That pure cold blessing of silence. Are you getting this. Are you keeping this. What we do this for. What we come down here for, Planky. No one else to see this. Far from the workaday world. Gas bills and nonsense. Just this. Purity and silence. Of course, of course. But none now the wrecked din of the skidoo a crashing noise a deafen din. Pollute. Still carve a graceful curve from the plateau down across the skiway and through the blind storm and on towards the cliffs of Priestley Head and so and so and work around towards dog leg of Lopez Sound and so on. Luke driving well. Take care and so on. The

77

crevices. Creases. Crevasses. Follow the bearing, take careful care in these conditions. Thomas sit tight now. They gather speed and come too close to Priestley Head the ground uneven and hidden rocks. Luke look Luke slow, too slow to warn or late to warn and now they hit a rock or crack or something frozen and in the air they lean and turn they fall is white is white they fall.

All slow and now the engine loud. All slow and now press face jacket crease squash face, fall, fall, snow. Weight. White. White. Heavy. White. Was up, was down. Heavy. White. Muffle. Muffle. Slow, slow. Think. Skidoo hit rock, turned over. Luke. Feeling gone right side face all down body. Falling. Weight. Silence. White. Mouth full. Snow pack tight. Wait. Up. Down. Floating. Low thing. Snow sling. Heart beat slow snow low light gone. Footsteps little far. Footsteps big near. Shout. Pull. Fight. Shout. Pull over, turn over. Breath. Big breath. Mouth open, cold air. Lungs burst. Breath, breath, breath. Stand. Lean. Fall.

Report making steady progress east to head of bay. Glacier. Crevasse. Snow thick driving hard again into. Wait. Incident report. Strike rock or crack or crest, turn over, engine pitch up up sky.

Arms hold. Lift. Voice talk. Luke talk. Talk nonsense words. Stand. Man grip a get now. Self on your now now. Grip on a get man your self come come. Get on a man grip your self now come.

Lean.

Luke ask question no sense words. So, so, so, low, so low so low. Slow. Slow. Sow. *Where – are – you – hurt?* Here. I am here. I am hurt here. Here is where I am. Here is where I am hurt. I am proceeding in a northerly direction nominally five metres above sea level. I am General Technical Assistant Robert Wright. I am hurt. I am he who is hurt. I am here. Numb the rub faith. The lips flap floppy and the words not come. The shapes. The face. Numb faith. Leg numb. Weak. Hold Luke. Hold. Lean. Fall.

Luke language and he turn around.

Luke putting the pup tent up. Good man, good man. Training. Remember training. Quick. Work quick. Heap snow on flap flaps pack down snow curing curing suck curing guys. Wind wild wild wind whirl whistle whistle whip. Drag him drag in him in tent. Heavy heavy heave ho heavy. Shut. Shut up. Shutter. Sheila. Shelter. Luke talk but no sense. What what wrong wrong. So low. Solo. Go slow. So low. Noise. Wide noise like apple oars. Apple sauce. Appley saws. Appley laws. Apple oars. Luke. Numb faith. Lips flop flappy. Numb faith. Say word jum jum jumper jump around word word. Luke say code. Talk. Luke say code. What. What. What. Face clothes. Clothes, clones, glows, near. Face near. Weather weather noise.

Luke say go for Thomas. He go. Walk. Far. But walk. Thomas.

Stop, stop. Risk. Stop. Think. Grip a get. Too far. Storm, storm. Gone now, man, gone. Thomas gone. Say close, here. Now. Stay here. Be serve. Preserve.

Luke say go, he go. In sub. Stub. Stubborn. Sub ordinated. Thomas still chance good chance help come.

Late, late, too late. Experience. Listen, experience. Get a man now. Remain in situ. Order, order. Express. Words come heavy and words not come.

Weather weather noise. Wild. Warm. Sleep. Slow. Blood pulse. Luke face close say words. Question. Crack. Gap. Train station upstate. Wanter un a hound is for. Want purse, purse, he. He, on, counted floor. Words wrong and unaccounted. Oh four. Oh four.

Warm. Sleep. Slow. Weather.

Luke say stay now, stay here, Doc stay here. Help will come. Luke find Thomas and Doc stay here. Help. Obviously. Obviously. Help will come.

Nod, yes. Nod. Weather weather noise. Quiet. Breathe. Zip.

Luke gone. Thomas gone.

Steps. Quiet. Breathe. Hurt. Breathe. Quiet. Breathe. Anna. Breathe.

Warm. Sleep. Fall.

Fall.

FALL _

1 _

It's Robert. It's your husband. I'm sorry to wake you. We need you to come.

The phone was buzzing on the bedside table. She answered it before she was quite awake: it's Robert, Anna. Something's happened. We need you to. There was a crack in the curtains. The sky was dark. The man was talking about flights and passports.

Years, she'd waited for something like this. Her imagination churning in the months he was away. It was almost a relief, now. A bloody-minded satisfaction in getting it over with.

She called Bridget before she did anything. It's Robert. Sorry, I know it's early. Something's happened. They want me to go down there. Is he okay? He's in the hospital. In Santiago. They're saying a stroke. They want me there. I don't know what I should do. Oh God, Anna, just go. Just get there. Worry about everything else later. Just go.

She left quickly. She locked the front door. She left a coffee cup on the table. She packed clothes for warm weather. She packed her laptop and work diary, her passport, her phone, her purse. She wrote down the booking numbers for the tickets. She turned the heating off. It was still dark when the taxi arrived.

Dawn was starting to happen somewhere way off in the east, shining against the ditches and flooded fields.

In the taxi for some reason she thought about Tim's funeral. Years earlier. The children had been much younger then. There had been discussion about whether they should come. They'll need to learn what these things are about, sooner or later. I think before they can walk is rather soon? She wanted to be there for Bridget. She didn't want to have to look after them. I'll make sure they don't bother you; they'll be fine. They really won't, though. In the end her parents had the children, and she and Robert went to the funeral on their own.

She didn't know what had reminded her. The rough fabric of the car seat. The smell of the air freshener. The way the taxi driver wouldn't stop talking. He was telling her this route might seem longer but it would avoid the traffic queueing to get onto the M11. She'd be surprised how early the traffic built up these days. Was she going anywhere nice?

At the funeral all the men had talked about *Planky's* achievements. None of them had called him Tim. Bridget had stared at the floor. He understood the risks we all take down there. He died doing something he loved. Above all else he was a family man. The light in the church had been clear and sharp, coming down against the cool stonework from the high leaded windows. Anna had wanted them all to stop talking so they could just sit quietly for a time.

She was the first person Bridget had called, when she'd found out about Tim. It had been difficult to understand what she was saying. Anna had asked if Robert was okay. This was the wrong thing to have said.

The taxi driver was telling her that at this time of year there was always ice on these roads and you couldn't be too careful.

It's Robert. I'm sorry to wake you. We need you to come. It's your husband.

Husband had been a difficult word to get used to, at first. She had wondered who people were talking about. What does your husband do? All the way through university and into her first research posts she had planned not to marry. Bridget told her she'd meet someone who would change her mind, but Anna doubted it. All the men she met in Cambridge were too busy talking to change her mind about anything. Robert was an exception, of sorts. He had a lot to say but he also knew how to listen. He asked questions, and considered the answers with care. It was unusual. She noticed. Later – too late – she'd watched him perform this listening for other people and realised it was something he knew how to turn on and off.

Their first conversation was in a corner snug of the Red Lion. December 1984. She told him about her research in anthropogenic climate impacts, and about her ambitions in the field of oceanographic modelling. She had one drink too many, and then another. She couldn't stop looking at his hands. While they were talking it suddenly occurred to her that he was beautiful. It was such an odd thought to have. His eyes were very brown. When she asked about Antarctica he said he was pleased to support other people's research for a change, and not worry about the results. He'd done mountain guiding in Scotland, he said, and this was more or less the same. She said wasn't it colder, probably? He spent a lot of time talking about what he'd done there, while insisting there really wasn't much to tell. He said he was losing interest in his own PhD. When they got outside it was cold and there was a fleeting chance of snow.

I don't know that it was a date, exactly. We talked. Did he walk you home? We walked home in the same direction. Did he try and kiss you? Well, how do you mean *try*?

Bridget had a way of laughing that meant: I'm going to explain something to you now, chicken.

One evening after that, when he was walking her home again, she said she would like him to kiss her. He'd laughed, and then said he wasn't laughing, he was only surprised. This wasn't the way it was done, apparently. While they kissed his breathing quickened suddenly, and he made a noise in the back of his throat. She understood that she was doing this to him. That she was wanted. There was a deep thrill in it.

And when are you going to sleep with him? Do you actually want to, like? He was talking about my church last night. I tried to explain, but I think he thinks I'm too religious. As in, too pure. Well, you're religious at least. Yes, but not like that. I'm not a Catholic or anything. You idiot, what do you think Catholics have been up to all this time?

It had been more or less new to them both, as far as she could tell, and after the first time she said she imagined it would get better once they'd had a chance to practise. He'd thought she was joking, and laughed. And then when she hadn't laughed he'd been very quiet. She had said the wrong thing. She told him she'd had a nice time. She also said he had the nicest penis she'd ever seen. You idiot, Anna; you were supposed to say *biggest*.

She checked the flight times, again. Bridget had sent her a message. Santiago was seven thousand two hundred and fifty-five miles away. The time in Santiago was Greenwich minus three hours. The weather was mild.

The man from the Institute had talked about Robert having *a bit of a stroke*. She knew that he'd meant to say *massive*, or *catastrophic*, or *dangerous*, because they were putting her on the first available flight. They wouldn't fly her there for *a bit* of a stroke. People didn't always say what they wanted to say.

A stroke is a cerebral injury. A stroke is ischaemic or haemorrhagic. Clots or bleeding. In the cortex. Subdural. The window of opportunity for thrombolysis is within four or five hours of the stroke occurring. Vascular surgery may be required in some cases. She didn't know what time the stroke had occurred, or where. She texted Bridget and asked her to call the children, when it was a decent hour. She still called Frank and Sara *the children*. They'd been adults for several years.

In the airport, sounds came at her from unexpected directions. There were announcements, and people shouting. Shoes squeaking on the hard polished floor. Stand there. Turn around please. Empty your pockets. There was a long time to wait for her flight. It was eleven years since she'd last been on a plane.

It's Robert. It's your husband. We need you to come.

Women researchers who married were typically set back in their careers by ten years, she had told Bridget. There was data on this. But Robert was an outlier; or at least the context of their relationship was an outlier. He had taken a permanent technician job with the Institute, and would be away in Antarctica for months at a time, which would leave her with the space to get on with her own work. They could put off having children until much later, if at all. They wouldn't be one of those couples where the wife sees all her ambition shrink in the shadow of her husband. We'll be anomalous, she told Bridget. Anomalous? Yes. So, essentially, you're going to marry him on the basis that he won't be around much? Yes, Bridget, that's correct. What? Anna, you are fucking perfect. You are my hero. I should marry you myself. Well, I don't think that's possible.

She waited by the departure gate. She bought a coffee. There were planes dropping down from the sky, and moving slowly across the concrete. In the distance, more planes went up into the air. This flight would produce approximately two metric tonnes of CO_2 per passenger. There were texts from Frank, and from Sara, asking her to call. What's happened? How's Dad? What have they told you? She replied to say she would call when she got there. When she knew more.

Her phone would work in Santiago. Wherever she went in the world people could reach her by text, or email, or video call. Even the main Institute base at Bluff Point had wi-fi now. When Frank was born she'd had to wait for the news to reach Robert via radio relay, and wait again for a reply. He was deep in the field so they'd been reliant on Morse code, and limited to a hundred words. He hadn't needed them all, apparently.

The flight was scheduled to take eleven and a half hours. Conditions were good but the pilot anticipated some turbulence mid-flight. The woman in the seat beside her started talking about Santiago. She went every year. Had Anna been? She had family there. Did Anna have family there? She had to go to the Cerro San Cristóbal, the woman told her. And she'd love the Mercado Central. She'd have a wonderful time. Did she have plans? Anna told the woman that her husband had had a stroke and might be dead when she got to Santiago. The woman said she didn't know what to say.

At the funeral, people hadn't mentioned how Tim had died, or why he had been in Antarctica at all. They didn't mention that the fall hadn't killed him, or that he would have been conscious for some time before freezing to death. They didn't explain that it had taken a team of six people to recover his body. They avoided mentioning that the trip itself had been unnecessary. Many of them possibly didn't know. Bridget knew. For a long time she tried to keep it from her children, but eventually they also knew. Anna's children had questions, and they asked more of them each year, when Robert kept going back South. Would he come back this time, they asked? Is he safe? Why does he have to go?

These were the risks they all accepted, Robert told her. She had never accepted the risk. Bridget had never accepted the risk. He didn't understand, when she'd tried to explain this.

You knew this would be the case when you married him, remember? You said you would be an *anomaly*. Yes, but I anticipated a certain flexibility, in the event of, you know, two young children who won't sleep. This is what he does, Anna. You've no right to hold it against him. For crying out loud, *woman*. Was that an impression, Bridget? It was; I thought it was pretty good, myself.

The flight attendants brought more meals, and the computer animation on the screen showed an aeroplane arcing over the Atlantic. She thought of how many times Robert had taken this same flight, en route to Antarctica. She thought about him now in a hospital bed. A bit of a stroke. We need you to come. Other people would be panicking at this point, she imagined, or preparing themselves to grieve. She needed more information first. I'll update you as soon as I know.

In the arrivals hall at Santiago, she saw a man holding a sign with her name written on it. She recognised him from conferences at the Institute. He told her how sorry he was, and that his name was Brian. He told her that everyone was rooting for Robert. She didn't know what this meant. She looked at him. He was holding a clipboard, and had a pen attached to a long cord around his neck.

'We spoke on the phone,' he said. 'I called you. About Robert.'

'Yes,' she said. 'I know.'

They got into a taxi that smelled of cigarettes and deodorant. The traffic was slow, and moved abruptly in confusing directions. There were tall buildings, pavement kiosks, people waiting at crossings. She kept seeing a mountain or a forested hill in the gaps between the buildings. Her phone kept buzzing. Brian was talking. It was too late to go to the hospital. The evacuation had gone as well as could be expected. There was some frostbite but Brian didn't think they would amputate. He looked pleased. There were text messages from people who wanted to know things. She had no more information for them.

The hotel was small, with a bar and restaurant in the lobby. Brian took care of the checking in, and said he would be back in the morning. A young man called Andreas carried her suitcase to her room, and told her about breakfast. Andreas was a German name but he had grown up in the Czech Republic.

She undressed, and took a long shower. She didn't sleep. She read about stroke care pathways and recovery outcomes. She exchanged text messages with Bridget, who told her it was late and to get some sleep. From the window she could see a busy road, tall buildings, and clouds underlit by the glow of street lights.

When Brian had said it was too late to go to the hospital, he had meant too late in the evening. Not *too late*. It wasn't too late, yet.

She tried to sleep.

2 _

In the morning she woke and it happened again. It's Robert. It's your husband. A bit of a stroke. We need you to. She was in a hotel room. She was in Santiago. Breakfast would be served between 7 and 9.30 a.m. in the restaurant downstairs. The weather would be warm, and clear. Brian would pick her up at nine. Her phone was heavy with missed calls and messages. She sent texts to Sara, and Frank. Going to hospital soon. Will update you when I know.

Breakfast was toast, yoghurt with fresh fruit, and coffee. Andreas served the coffee with a complex shape drawn in the froth, and asked about her stay. He had several roles at the hotel. The traffic outside was heavy. A lorry strained through an awkward manoeuvre, belching black smoke as the driver crunched the gears. When Brian arrived he was still carrying the clipboard, and wearing the pen on a string around his neck. He stood in the lobby and waited for her to finish eating.

At the hospital he didn't know where to go. The signs were all in Spanish and every corridor looked the same. He apologised several times, and laughed. You wouldn't think I was only here yesterday, he said.

When they found the ward a nurse showed them to a bed beside a window. Robert was there. He had marks and bruises on his face. His hands were propped awkwardly across the top of the sheets, as though someone else had put them there. He looked at her, and his eyes closed slowly. She stood beside his bed. Somebody brought her a chair. She said his name, and he opened his eyes. She waited. He closed his eyes again.

People arrived, and told her things. Your husband is not well. He is not out of danger. We don't know yet the extent. For now we must just wait to see. A nurse squeezed past and slipped a blood pressure cuff around Robert's arm. He opened his eyes to see what she was doing. She inflated the cuff with one hand, looking at her watch. Another nurse brought a syringe and drew blood, wiping a clean spot on Robert's arm and easing the needle in.

'*Bueno, gracias,*' she said, softly. He nodded very slightly and went back to sleep.

Brian asked if there was anything else he could do, and Anna said she had some questions about what had actually happened down there. They were still piecing things together, he told her. There was some uncertainty. They were still pinning things down. He didn't look her in the eye. He spoke slowly, and sometimes he stopped and changed what he was saying. She wondered about the word *pinning*.

Robert had been part of a small team at Station K., he said. There had been bad weather while they were out in the field. Navigational issues. The team had become separated, and there were some communication difficulties. When the search party arrived from Bluff Point, Robert was found to have symptoms consistent with a stroke, and his immediate evacuation had been prioritised.

'Wait.'

'I know this must be difficult for you, Anna. The Institute will do everything we can.'

'Wait, the others. How many were there? Are they all okay?'

'Two. There are two. Younger colleagues.'

'And they're okay? They're back at Bluff Point?'

'Their location has been confirmed. We're waiting for a break in the weather to get a plane in.'

'They're still down there? Are they back in the hut? They're not out in the field, surely?'

The situation was developing quickly, he told her. One member of the team had been recovered in the near vicinity of Robert, and escorted to the field hut. He was helping to coordinate matters. A second plane had been en route but the weather had deteriorated fast. If Anna needed anything else she could contact him. He was looking at her. This meant he was waiting for her to speak. She didn't have anything else to say. He said he would be back later.

She sat beside Robert's bed and waited. The light from the window moved across his face. The clouds moved across the sky. Bridget couldn't believe the two boys were still down there. Something must have gone seriously wrong. Let me see what I can find out. Let me know if you want to talk. Robert's breathing was steady and shallow and the muscles in his face were still. People came and checked his blood pressure, his heart rate, his breathing. They changed the bags of glucose solution on his drip. They turned his body and washed it and touched it all over. She watched and she waited and sometimes she stepped out of the way. His breathing was steady and shallow. His hands on the bedcovers were still. The effects of stroke include language impairments, reduced mobility, difficulties with swallowing, and cognitive deficits. The risk of further stroke is high. The cerebrovascular accident has occurred in the left frontoparietal region. Your husband is a very lucky man. When we consider the circumstance. On the scan we see the damage on the left side, here. We see dead tissue but also a penumbra and this can be saved. As the swelling subsides we will see much recovery. We can expect that his language will affect in some way.

She said his name and he opened his eyes. She reached out for his hand and asked if he could hear her. Did he know where they were? Could he nod, or squeeze her hand? He blinked in a way that might or might not have been deliberate, and closed his eyes.

A cleaner in a brown tunic moved between the beds, wiping down the handrails, the chairs, the bedside lockers, the frames of the beds and the machines around them. She had a system of coloured cloths too complex to follow.

Robert opened his eyes, and looked at her.

A young woman walked through the ward and stopped beside the bed opposite Robert's. She carefully rolled her sleeves to her elbows before leaning over the bed and embracing a much older man. As she stood back, the man sank into the pillows and nodded several times.

There were fragments of explanations. Everyone assumed she'd already been told something by somebody else. People talked about procedures and possible outcomes as if this was something she'd been through before. The doctors had a habit of touching her arm when they'd finished their explanations. The nurses checked Robert's pulse, and his blood pressure. Two porters arrived, and wheeled him away in his bed.

There was another text from Bridget. There had been nothing in the news about the two boys, and the people she knew at the Institute were being tight-lipped. It didn't sound great.

Tight-lipped meant they weren't saying anything.

Sara called. She had been trying to get hold of her. Was there something wrong with her phone? What would happen now? Anna told her that Robert would be okay. He probably wasn't going to die, she clarified. His long-term recovery was impossible to predict at this stage. Sara made noises that may have been crying. It was hard to tell, with the noise of the traffic. She just couldn't believe it. Anna said she would call later but she was at the hospital now.

There were emails from work. The director of research wanted to *bring her up to speed* with the latest preparations for the REF submission. She also wanted to know if Anna would be able to attend the next meeting.

Frank called for an update. She told him that Robert had been taken for another scan. Should Frank come to Santiago, he wanted to know. Did he need to be there? He seemed to be implying an important question but she didn't know what it was.

When they brought Robert back he was sitting up in the bed, with extra pillows propped behind him. He looked at her, and twisted his mouth into half a smile. She leaned towards him, looking into his eyes. His mouth opened and closed. She rested her hands on his, and kissed the side of his face. He had a different smell. She stepped back. His eyes were roaming. She said hello; it was all she could think to say. His mouth opened and closed. He pulled his lips back, and she didn't know if he was trying to smile or wincing in pain or what he was trying to say.

She asked if he was okay. She asked if he felt any different. She asked if he knew how long he'd been here. His eyes roamed over her face, and around the room. She asked if he could understand what she was saying. He said nothing. She held his hands in hers. She waited.

'Whuh.'

'What's that? Robert?'

'Whuuuh.'

'Robert?'

A nurse came over, and said something in Spanish. She pointed at Robert's mouth, and then put a hand over her own.

'*No hablar*,' she said. '*Sin palabras.*'

Something about words. Not speaking. Anna smiled, and said thank you. Robert's hands felt restless beneath hers. His mouth opened and closed. There were sounds.

'We're in Santiago, Robert. They got you out. You were in trouble, I think.'

'Whuh.'

'Okay? They got you out.'

'Wh—'

'Robert? We'll be going home, soon, when you're ready.'

'Wh, whuh. Whuuuh.'

—

In the morning she woke while it was still dark. It's your husband. It's Robert. Something's happened. A stroke is a cerebral injury. We must wait for the swelling. He's not speaking. It's not possible to know the extent. Not yet. They haven't said. For now we must just wait to see. There are numerous assessment and intervention strategies available to the person with aphasia.

Downstairs the restaurant was empty. The traffic moved thickly through the street outside. She looked at the map on her phone, working out a route to the hospital. She saw the Mercado Central. She wondered if there was a Meeting House here, and if she might find the time to go. Andreas brought coffee, and asked about her husband. He had worked at the hotel for three years now. He had been taught how to draw shapes in the latte froth by his ex-boyfriend. He said that it was more for affect than effect.

She walked to the hospital, and checked her messages. Any news? Have you spoken to the doctors today? Has Frank called? Anna, do you want me to liaise with the rest of the family? So sorry to hear. Please let us know. Keep us updated. Do let us know if there's anything we can do.

The hospital wasn't as far as Brian had said it would be. When she got to the ward, one of the nurses was washing Robert in his bed. Anna could hear her murmuring to Robert while she worked, telling him what she was doing. She was speaking in Spanish; something like *girar un poco*, and *lavarse el trasero*. It was difficult to make out the words. Robert's eyes were half closed, but he opened them occasionally and gazed at the woman. There was an easy strength in the way she lifted Robert's limbs, and rolled him onto his side. A complete lack of inhibition in the way she touched him. Anna would be doing these things herself, soon.

There was a commotion at the desk. A woman was holding two large bouquets of flowers, and a nurse was trying to take them away. There were loud voices in Spanish, and the woman with the flowers kept lifting them out of reach of the nurse. Other nurses got involved, and the conversation moved into the corridor. The voices grew softer.

There were more emails from her colleague, asking if she could run the reports on the last sets of data they'd been working on. She understood this was a difficult time but the team were relying on her input. The Montreal conference was coming up fast.

A speech therapist arrived to assess Robert. She asked him to stick out his tongue, and he looked at her blankly until she stuck out her own. She asked him to puff out his cheeks, showing him how and then holding her fingers up to his lips. She told him he was doing well. Anna had no idea what he was doing well. He looked at Anna with an expression she couldn't read. The woman offered him a drink of water, holding a stethoscope against his throat while he took a small sip. She asked him to take another sip. She glanced up at the ceiling while she listened to him swallow. She nodded, and put the stethoscope away. She asked questions, and made notes when he replied. Some of the questions were unexpected. She asked if his name was Pedro, and when he said *whur* she asked if he could nod the head or shake the head. Your name is Pedro? His eyes roamed around the room. She asked if his name was Robert, and his attention clicked back to her. He dropped and lifted his head, and brought his hand to his chest.

'Wuurr.'

'Your name is Robert?'

'Wuurr.'

'Good. Okay. Robert.'

She wrote something down. He watched her. His fingers were tip-tapping on the bedsheets. She asked if they were in a hotel. He looked at her, waiting. She asked if they were in a hospital. He dropped his head sharply, and lifted it. This was his nod, now.

'Wuur.'

'*Bueno, bueno*. Very good. Okay.'

She asked if he was in the bed, and he nodded. She pointed at Anna, and asked if this lady was Robert's father. Robert barked out a single, hard laugh. Is she a wife? He nodded.

'Okay, good. Now. I want you to follow the instruction. Can you touch your nose, Robert? Yes? Put your fingers on your nose?'

He could. Slowly, he brought his hand towards his face, and found his nose. He seemed surprised it was there.

'Can you point to the ceiling?'

He waved his hand in the air, still looking at the woman.

'Can you touch your head, and then point to your wife?'

He looked at Anna. His hand lifted, and dropped. He moved his eyes from side to side. A series of expressions moved across his face, refusing to settle. The woman made some notes.

'Okay. I want you to touch your knee after you turn to the window.'

He looked at her. He jerked his head. He made an angry face, and noises in the back of his throat. The woman put a hand out towards him and said it was okay, he was tired now, she would come back. Robert let his weight settle back into the pillows, and his eyes fell immediately closed.

The nurses came and checked his blood pressure, his heart rate, his breathing. They lifted his arms and scratched his feet and asked him to swallow water. She watched, and she waited. She tried to work. She got distracted. Aphasia is the name given to a wide range of language deficits caused by damage to the brain. Deficit can be expressive or receptive. Rates and degrees of recovery vary and are difficult to predict. The weather was clear and hot. Bridget was there if she wanted to talk. Any time. His breathing was steady and shallow. He looked at her, his mouth opening and closing, his eyes roaming around the room.

Bridget always wanted her to talk. She was under the impression that Anna *bottled things up*. It went right back to when they'd first become friends. You can tell me anything, Anna, I'm a good listener. Aren't you meant to stop talking, to be a good listener? There's no point me stopping until you get started, chicken. There's no point me starting when you're such good value. Very true; have I told you about the new boy? Dean? God no! I mean Plank. He's not much of a conversationalist but he's a monster in the sack. He's a what in the what?

An assistant in a pale yellow tunic moved through the ward with a trolley, replacing jugs of water and taking away empty cups and saucers.

Sara called, and asked if she was okay. Why hadn't Anna answered her calls? Anna told her that Robert was in good hands. Did she know when they might be coming home? Anna didn't imagine it would be very soon. Sara was having a problem at work. She was worried that some things she'd said may have been misunderstood. She should talk to her line manager, Anna said. Sara made some noises that sounded like she was arguing with someone else in the room.

Brian came to the ward and asked how Robert was doing. Everyone at the Institute sent their very best wishes. There was something he needed to say. Anna asked what it was. Did he have any update on Robert's colleagues? He did. This was what he had come to discuss with them both. He was terribly sorry. He had been asked to speak to Robert in person. Before *mumble mumble*. Anna asked him to repeat himself. Something was wrong. It had taken longer than anticipated to locate and you could say extract the second of Robert's colleagues. He had very unfortunately passed, which is, passed away, during the flight back to Bluff Point.

Robert tried to lean forward, grappling at the rail of his bed. He made a noise across his bottom lip: *fuarr, farr*.

They were still waiting to inform family members before they could release any more information. He was very sorry to be the bearer of such bad, as it were, *news*.

Anna asked what had, in fact, what the hell had actually happened. Her voice was louder than she'd intended. Brian said how sorry he was, he understood that this was, he wanted, obviously everything had.

They were still working to establish the facts.

3 —

In the morning she was woken by her phone. She stared up at the ceiling as it buzzed and skittered around on her bedside table. She didn't want to look at it. She reached over and covered it with a cushion. She could still hear it rattling, and she held the cushion down until it stopped.

It's your husband. It's Robert. Something's happened. A stroke is a cerebral injury. We must wait for the swelling. He's not speaking. It's not possible to know the extent. Not yet. They haven't said. For now we must just wait to see. There are numerous assessment and intervention strategies available to the person with aphasia. We really need to get your comments on the draft paper before tomorrow's deadline. Bridget had just heard about Thomas. So awful. So sorry. How's Robert? Anna didn't know who Thomas was. Robert's colleague. One of them had unfortunately passed. The BBC site was reporting a tragic accident in Antarctica. Thomas Myers was a mapping specialist. The report mentioned navigational difficulties. It mentioned the medical evacuation of an older colleague. It detailed the Institute's excellent safety record, noting that the last death had been in 1998. There was a picture of Tim Carruthers.

Frank called while she was on her way to the hospital. He wanted to know what had happened. Does Dad know? Has he told you? Who has he talked to? Anna asked him to slow down. She reminded him that Robert wasn't telling anyone anything. What have they asked him? What have they told you? Don't let him talk to anyone, Frank said. Don't even let him say he's sorry.

Anna looked at the phone, wondering if it was working properly. He can't talk to anyone, she said again. No, Mum, he can't; don't let him, okay?

On the ward, a nurse showed Anna how to spoon food into Robert's mouth. The food was mashed, and smelled of banana. Robert chewed slowly and awkwardly, and some of the mush spilled from his mouth. The nurse wiped it away with a napkin. '*Un poco*,' she said. Her name was Rosanna. She had been working on the ward for seven years. *Un poco* meant a little. She cleaned Robert's face again, and left them. Robert looked at Anna, and at the bowl, and raised his eyebrows. He made a noise in the back of his throat. A small growl or a groan. When he had finished eating she told him it was Thomas who had died at Station K. He looked at her. Thomas Myers, she said. Thomas. He made a puffing sound, biting at his bottom lip. She asked if he had known him well. She asked what had happened. He looked at her, and screwed up as much of his face as he was able to move.

Two physiotherapists arrived. They wanted to run through some exercises with Robert. They raised the head of his bed to a sitting position, and stood on either side of him. They asked him to lift up his arm, higher, higher, and the other arm. Stretch your fingers. Push your hand against my hand. Harder, harder. Hold this cup in your left hand. And in your right hand. No, okay.

They lifted the bedcovers and told him to move his feet, move his toes, lift one leg and the other leg. They wrote things down. They told him this was enough now, good work, rest now and they would come back tomorrow and stand him.

A cleaner in a brown tunic moved through the wards with a laundry trolley, dropping a stack of fresh sheets and pillowcases onto the table beside each bed. The light and the long shadows moved across the floor. Bridget sent her love, again, and a promise of wine as soon as she was home. She'd been to check on the house. Anna told her she was fine, that she was back at the hospital, that Robert was sleeping.

Brian came to the ward and talked about an investigation. He seemed not to understand Robert's communication deficits, and when he didn't get an answer he simply asked the same question again, louder and more slowly. The surviving colleague was a young man called Luke. Luke *Adebayo*, which Brian made a show of pronouncing. He was recuperating in the medical room at Bluff Point, and would be likely to return to Cambridge with the next transport flight. He had been kept up to date on Robert's condition.

We must just wait to see.

The speech therapist came back. Her name was Julia. She lived on the north side of the city, and it took her an hour to drive in every day. She had a file of notes, and a folder with laminated picture cards and word lists. She had found English translations of her resources online, she said. She held up a picture of a cat.

'Is this a cat, Robert?'

'Yeth. Yeth. Yes.'

'Very good. Can you say *cat*?'

Robert opened his mouth and made a retching sound, as though he were choking on the word. Julia nodded, wrote something down, and held up a picture of a ship.

'Is this a shoe? A *shoe*, Robert?'

'Ssh. Yes. Sshh.'

'This is something that floats on the water, Robert. Does a shoe float?'

'Shhh.'

'Is this a ship?'

'Yes!'

'Ship. Good. Ssh – ship.' She made more notes. She turned to Anna, suddenly, and smiled. She held up a picture of an aeroplane.

'Puh–puh–puh.'

'You can say this already?'

'Pay-lane. Red. Red pay-lane.'

'Plane? Yes. Aeroplane, very good.'

'Red pay-lane.'

The aeroplane in the picture was blue. Julia ignored this, and moved on. She held up pictures of balloons, cows, cars, and radios, and watched him trying to shape his mouth around the words, or not knowing even what word to attempt. She made notes, and said she would be back tomorrow. Robert fell asleep.

On the other side of the ward, the smart young woman with the rolled-up sleeves was sitting beside the older man's bed. She was reading a magazine, but she kept putting it down to do something with her phone. Occasionally while she typed a smile broke out across her face. Whenever it did, she covered her mouth with her hand until her usual taut expression returned.

Anna went to the cafeteria, and tried to work. She had turned on her out-of-office, but there were still emails that couldn't wait. There were PhD supervisions to rearrange, and a slightly panicked-sounding email from a research associate about a missed allocation on the server. There was a deadline coming up on a major funding application, and her colleague needed filling in on the details if she was going to take over the writing. There would be teaching cover to arrange. The students were so committed to their studies, and so impatient to move into research. She wondered what they might achieve. They could only establish the same things all over again, with ever-increasing certainty and detail. Yes, there is a clear link between CO_2 emissions and temperature rise. No, there is no historical precedent. Yes, immediate action is required.

When she got back to the ward the curtains around Robert's bed were closed. A high-pitched alarm was quietly beeping. She could hear people behind the curtains, moving around his bed, talking quickly to each other. A nurse took her arm and showed her to a chair.

'Here, you wait,' she told Anna. 'It will be okay.'

—

In the morning she went to a Friends Meeting House she had found online. It was in a room above a menswear shop, with walls of bare plaster and a small circle of wooden chairs. She sat and waited. There were three other people. There were flowers in a tall vase by the window, and when a lorry went past outside they trembled. Her breathing slowed. Two more people arrived. The light on the floor shifted around as the curtains moved in the breeze. After half an hour or so an elderly man stood, carefully, and spoke in English, with an accent she thought might be from Texas, or Florida. He said something about the call to wait. It was a call to action like any other, he said. She didn't really know what he meant. She often didn't know what people meant when they spoke in meetings. She liked the idea of them speaking more than what they had to say. And she liked the silence. It was a year or so since she'd last been to a meeting. She'd long ago fallen out of the habit of going; Robert had never been interested, and the children had struggled when she'd tried to bring them along, and so it had become something in the background. Something she would get back to, one day. She'd missed it, she realised. She didn't know why she hadn't gone back once the children had left home. She sat, and listened to the traffic outside. She shifted in her seat. At the end of the meeting people shook hands and she slipped away.

Outside, a man standing beside a barrow piled high with oranges said something to her in Spanish. She watched his mouth moving. She said, '*Gracias*,' and walked on.

When she got to the ward, Robert was sitting on the edge of his bed, with a physiotherapist on either side and a walking frame in front of him. They each had an arm around his waist. He was listening to them intently. Anna watched. Slowly, they guided him to a standing position. The strength was almost all theirs. His legs trembled. His whole body shook. The physiotherapists spoke to each other in Spanish, and said Robert's name over and over. When he was close to upright they guided his hands to the walking frame. He shouted out in pain or exhilaration and they carefully lowered him back to the bed.

Overnight a young man had arrived in the bed opposite Robert's. He had a tube in his nose and an oxygen tank beside the bed, and the right side of his body was restless. He made groaning noises and occasionally shouted. The nurses watched, and left him alone.

Rosanna came and took Robert's blood pressure, and wrote numbers down on his chart. Another nurse came and gave him his medication. He was able to swallow tablets now, which meant fewer injections. The needles had left bruises all along his arms. He looked at Anna and tried to smile. There was a focus in his eyes that hadn't been there before. His speech wasn't returning but he was starting to follow the pattern of conversation.

'They work you hard in here, don't they?'

'Wuur. Yes. Yes obs-feesly.'

'Bet you'd rather be back at Station K.'

'Wuur! Christ.'

'At least you'd get some peace and quiet.'

'Well, obsvially. Of course. Yet.'

'*Yes.*'

'Yes, yes.'

'I spoke to Sara.'

'Wuur?'

'She's okay. She's having some trouble at work. Something about feeling undermined. I don't know.'

'Yes, yes. Christ.'

'I know. She just needs to find the right job. I'm not sure she's cut out for. For.'

'Wuur?'

'No. I'm not sure what it is she does either. Brand strategy? Digital brand strategy?'

'Yes, yes.'

'Do you remember when she wanted to be a doctor?'

'Wuur.'

'Might have come in handy.'

'Haaaarr.'

'Frank texted as well.'

'Yes, yes.'

'I mean. You know. Everyone's been texting. Frank wants me to put him on a video call when the doctor speaks to us next. He says he wants to hear for himself. He wants to know what the plans are.'

'Pah, lans.'

'Very good. *Plans.*'

'Pah, lans.'

'I've told him there aren't really any plans, but he still wants to get involved.'

'Yes, yes. Well obviously, of course.'

'Of course.'

A nurse came to remove Robert's catheter, and show him how to use a bedpan. She closed the curtains and pulled back the covers. She was talking to them both. It was uncomfortable watching the nurse handle Robert's penis, but she tried to concentrate. The end of his penis was bruised. The nurse wanted him to go there and then, but he was clearly too embarrassed. Anna found the embarrassment reassuring.

—

In the morning she woke and she was still in Santiago. Robert was still in the hospital. The boy he had been responsible for was still dead. At breakfast she went through her emails. There was a booking confirmation from the airline, which she assumed was a mistake. Andreas brought coffee, and toast. The booking system had automatically generated a return journey, perhaps. She would ask Brian to resolve the issue. Andreas brought fresh fruit, and asked about Robert.

At the hospital Brian introduced a young woman in a zip-up fleece as Kirsty. Kirsty was a doctor with the Institute. She looked very young. Anna held out her hand and said hello. Kirsty said she'd be overseeing the repatriation, and would travel with Robert. The word *repatriation* took a moment to register. Anna asked what she meant, and Kirsty explained that *repatriation* simply referred to the transfer of a patient to their home country.

'No, sorry, I know what the word means. I'm asking when are you talking about this happening? When was this decided?'

Kirsty made a face, and turned to Brian. Brian said that arrangements had been made for transfer to the Stroke Unit in Cambridge, and he thought this had all been discussed. Anna said that no, it really hadn't.

'Yeth, yeth,' Robert said. 'Huh, huh. Huh-ma.'

Anna told him he wasn't going home, not yet. Just to the hospital in Cambridge. She was suddenly very tired. He wasn't ready, surely. She said this to Brian, or Kirsty, and they both said he was doing really well. He was out of danger. He was fit enough to travel and would do better in a British hospital, in a familiar environment. I thought we would be here for weeks, Anna said, and Brian apologised. He thought this had all been explained.

'Right. Kirsty, was it?'

'Yes. I'm a doctor with the Institute, with the medical section.'

'Yes, Brian just said. Can I ask, were you involved? Were you there?'

'With Robert? I was involved in the operation, yes.'

'You found him?'

'Yes.'

'What happened?'

Kirsty turned to Brian before she answered. It was a tiny movement and she tried to hide it, but Anna saw. She didn't know what it meant, but she saw. When Kirsty answered, her voice took on a rehearsed quality. She talked about the first confirmation of location, the reduced visibility, the lack of radio communication, the challenging landing. His location at the skiway made a lot of difference, she said. They weren't sure how but he'd made his way there from a tent about five hundred metres away. Brian was looking at his phone while they were talking, and off towards the ward entrance. Kirsty said that Robert's right-sided weakness had immediately suggested a cerebral injury. She hesitated, and then clarified that she meant a *stroke*, and Anna told her that, again, the clarification wasn't necessary.

'There was a lot we needed to do, and we couldn't do most of it until we'd got him to a proper medical facility. Two of my colleagues stayed with Luke to continue the search for Thomas. There was a second team on the way. We had to get Robert out as quickly as possible. He was very cold, of course. Minimally responsive. But he did well. He was very brave, weren't you, Robert?'

Robert looked at her. Brian said they should be getting on. He said he'd update her *as soon as poss*. The ward was quiet for a moment after they'd left. Anna looked at Robert.

'I, bruuurr,' he said.

'Exactly, Robert, brave. Bruuur. Such a brave boy. Well done.'

She sent messages to Frank and Sara, and Bridget, to let them know. Frank asked for the details of her flight. Bridget said she would make a lasagne. In the hospital shop she bought a box of chocolates and a card for the nursing staff. She only knew three of their names. She took them to the ward, and told Robert she would see him back in Cambridge. He tried to say something about a plane, lifting his hand through the air. Yes, she agreed; he'd be going on a plane.

She went back to the hotel and packed. Andreas arranged a taxi for her, and while they waited for it to arrive he asked if she had enjoyed her stay. She looked at him.

'I'm sorry,' he said. 'My thinking is pre-empted by my speaking, sometimes.'

'That can be a problem, Andreas.'

'I hope your husband is well soon.'

'Thank you. And I hope—'

'Your taxi is here.'

The taxi smelled of cigarettes and air freshener. She opened the window and the warm evening air pillowed in. The driver pressed a button and the window closed again.

The airport was almost empty, and bigger than she remembered. She walked through metal detectors and emptied her pockets. Somebody asked if she wanted to buy perfume. Frank texted to say he would meet her at the airport.

When the plane took off, the seat beside her was still empty. She was grateful for this. The flight attendant served dinner, and asked if everything was okay for her. Had she enjoyed her stay? Anna had seen almost nothing of the city while she'd been there. She hadn't been to the Mercado Central, or the Cerro San Cristóbal. She hadn't eaten conger eel soup or empanadas. Everything was okay, she told the attendant. Thank you. Everything was fine.

—

Frank met her in the arrivals hall, and drove her home. The weather was a shock, after Santiago. As they walked through the car park the air felt damp against her skin. The tops of the street lights vanished into a fog. There were a lot of cars in the car park. Bridget wanted to know when she could come over. Sara wanted to know when Anna would call.

Frank drove quickly, but well. He didn't listen to music, and he concentrated on what the other drivers were doing. He asked what Santiago had been like, and she said she didn't really know.

'I only saw the hospital, and the hotel.'

'Right. Of course.'

'And I went to meeting, once.'

'You still go?'

'Yes.'

'You still believe that stuff?'

'I don't think believing is relevant. I like going to meetings.'

'Sure. Fine.'

114

They were driving north, and the sun was setting. The fields were empty and dark on either side of the road. Frost capped the ploughed ridges. Low clouds streaked towards the horizon. Behind them the night was coming in. They could see the house while they were still a long way off, a low silhouette against the sky. For some reason the lights had been left on.

4 _

She had bought the house on her own, while Robert was away. It hadn't been a rash decision, but she'd made it quickly and it hadn't occurred to her to ask what he thought. She had always taken pride in being able to do things alone, while he was gone. It was part of the arrangement. We're going to be an anomaly. My husband's away. He left in November and he came back in March, and it just became the rhythm of their life together. She was surprised, the first time he came back, by the hunger she felt for him. For his body; for the sound of his voice. She hadn't noticed missing him while he was gone. In later years this hunger declined, but it never quite went away.

On two occasions he stayed away for the whole year, supporting work in a deep field camp during the long Antarctic winter. She liked being able to say that her husband was *away in Antarctica*. It sounded glamorous. Heroic, on both their parts. She secured a permanent research post at the university, and published several well-received papers. It became known that she was often on her own, and the younger members of the department included her in their socialising. On two occasions this socialising had led to a man ending up in her bed. Both experiences had been very pleasant, but she hadn't thought it worth the complication of continuing. Bridget didn't know about these occasions; Anna imagined she would be surprised.

She came down in the morning and found all the post stacked on the kitchen table. Frank must have put it there. It took her a moment to understand what it was. Her body was still vibrating from the long flight home. Frank was asleep in the spare room. It was dark outside. She made a pot of tea, and sat at the table. She sorted the handwritten envelopes from the bills and junk mail, and started to read. So sorry to hear about. So sorry to hear. Do wish him well. Get well soon. A very good colleague. Hope he'll be back soon. Our thoughts and prayers. This was what happened when someone died, she supposed. Condolences. Unfamiliar handwriting. People searching for the right words, and not always finding them.

There had been a stack of cards like this when they'd married and moved into their first home. Congratulations, mostly, and good luck. That tiny cottage hidden in the trees, with the garden running down to the stream. The table that took up the whole kitchen. She hadn't understood the *luck*, then. The one bedroom at the top of the narrow stairs, and the bathroom backing out into the garden. It wasn't big enough for a family, but after Frank was born she'd put off doing anything about it. She'd done so much work on the place that she was reluctant to leave: straightening the wonky cupboard doors, fixing the light switches that fizzed when she turned them on, screwing down the creaking stairs. She'd partitioned their bedroom to create a sleeping alcove for Frank. She'd built a fence at the end of the garden, the day after Frank fell face first into the stream and she'd yanked him out by his hair before even registering what was happening. But when she discovered she was pregnant with Sara, not long after Robert had gone South again, she sold it and bought a new house without even writing to let Robert know.

The new house was damp, exposed to the wind, and barely above nineteenth-century sea levels, let alone those that were coming in the twenty-first. It wasn't on a bus route, and it wasn't near a school. It was twenty minutes' drive from Bridget's house. It was a poorly supported decision. But there was a bedroom for each of the children, and a door that opened directly from the kitchen into the garden – and that garden had fruit trees, and compost bins, and an uninterrupted view of fields and trees all the way to the horizon, and whenever she came home to see the lights spilling out into the darkness she knew she'd done the right thing.

She heard movements upstairs. She finished her first cup of tea. Outside, the darkness gave way to a thin white mist. She could see the outline of the damson tree at the end of the garden, and little else. A muffled red glow along the horizon, from the traffic on the A14.

Robert is a respected colleague. We hope he'll be back with us soon.

The children had always been wary when Robert came back from Antarctica. It was only natural, after four or five months away, but it took him by surprise every time. If he tried to pick them up they would wriggle to be put down, and she would have to say they were just tired. He would remind her how important his work was, and that he couldn't help having to be away. She had to reassure him, and reassure them, and persuade them to spend time with the man they'd got used to not having around.

But by primary school age they were proud of him, and of what he did, and from what she could gather they often showed off about him at school. They didn't show off about her building sophisticated oceanographic computer models, apparently. Perhaps no one asked. Frank's bedroom in particular was full of the artefacts Robert brought back: the compasses and ice axes, the maps and charts on the wall. And they started to hear things from their friends about what a dangerous place it must be. They ask, every time, if he's going to be okay, she told Bridget. Sure, and you tell them of course he is? Well, I tell them there are substantial risks but he's being very careful. Jesus, Anna, you're supposed to lie to your kids about this stuff, don't you think? I hardly think that's appropriate, Bridge.

As teenagers they became more resentful. They asked her, several times, what the point of him was. Sara once urged her to get divorced. And then suddenly they were gone, Frank first and then Sara, and when Robert went South again she had the whole house to herself. She got used to the silence again, in his absence. She started noticing just how much Robert talked when he was there. They argued about it sometimes. He said she'd used to like hearing what he had to say. And when he was packing for this trip, back in October, there had been a particularly long story about the new colleagues he would be working with, and something that had happened at the training conference, and when she left the room while he was still talking he just followed her. She'd snapped.

When she told Bridget the story later it sounded like a joke. You've never been that good at swearing, chicken. *Shut the shit*

119

up? I don't know if that's even a thing. Well it worked anyway, Bridge. He did shut the shit up. I never heard the end of the story. Stony silence. He left early in the morning.

It couldn't have been the actual last thing she'd said to him; not quite. But it felt like it.

—

Frank started talking before he even appeared in the room. He wanted to know what Robert had told her about *the incident*.

'Well, he hasn't told me anything. He's had a stroke, Frank. He can barely speak.'

'Jesus, Mum, yes. But he can still communicate, right? He can nod and shake his head? I'm just wondering what they've asked him; what he's agreed to.'

'He can't shake his head, actually. He can't say no.'

'What?'

'He just kind of waves his hand in front of his face, when he means no.'

'Wow. Right. But that's consistent?'

'No,' she said. 'Nothing's consistent, really.'

He helped himself to breakfast, and told her he'd drive them both to the hospital. Had anyone from the Institute been asking Robert questions? Had they offered him any legal support? Anna said she would prefer to get the bus, and asked why Robert would need legal support. Frank was driving anyway. He didn't have time for her to be a martyr about it. Something had gone wrong, and Robert had been responsible.

'Responsible?'

'I don't mean *responsible* like it was his fault. I mean, shit, I hope not. I mean responsible like: he was in a position of *responsibility*, right? He's vulnerable, Mum. If this kid's parents sue the Institute, Dad's right in the front line.'

Anna started getting her things together. She reminded Frank about all the disclaimers that people signed when they worked for the Institute. They understood the risks, she said.

'Now you sound like Dad.'

'I'm just saying. There were unforeseen circumstances. No one's going to blame him.'

'You should get the house put in your name, Mum.'

'What are you talking about?'

'The house. Assets. You need to take some precautions.'

'Well. I hardly think. I just.'

'Shall we go?'

'Yes. Okay. Fine.'

—

Someone had cut Robert's hair, and trimmed his beard. It was difficult to know how they'd found the time, when he'd been there for barely twenty-four hours. His bed was at the far end of the ward. There was a window but it looked directly onto a brick wall. She reached out and ran her hand across Robert's head. This wasn't the way he liked it. It was too short. There was no shape. He looked at her and nodded. A woman appeared and said she was the nurse-in-charge. She started talking about visiting hours and named doctors and SLTs, and Anna interrupted to ask who had cut his hair. The hairdresser came through once a fortnight, the nurse-in-charge said. Robert had said it was fine to go ahead. They actually had a great deal of experience in communicating with their patients, and if he'd had any objections he would have been able to let them know. Anna asked Robert if he was happy with it.

'Yes, yes,' he said. 'Obviously, of course.' He grabbed her hand and pulled it against his cheek. The beard was cut almost to stubble. She hadn't seen it like this since they were students. He looked at her, raising his eyebrows.

Frank touched her shoulder, and said that the nurse was asking if she had any more questions.

Another nurse appeared with a blood pressure monitor on wheels. She wrapped the cuff around Robert's arm and pressed some buttons. The cuff inflated automatically. Robert widened his eyes. The nurse asked if Robert had any pains or discomfort, and Robert said obviously, of course, of course.

'He has trouble saying no,' Anna told the nurse.

'Well, obviously,' Robert said.

'Robert, can you say yes if you have any pain?'

He looked at them both, blinking. The blood pressure monitor beeped several times, and the nurse wheeled it away. Outside in the car park there were cars driving in circles, looking for spaces, their headlights swinging through the mist. Frank was busy doing something on his phone, walking backwards and forwards through the ward. Anna asked Robert how the flight had been. How was the lovely young Kirsty? Robert smiled, opening and closing his mouth quickly, making jabbering sounds. Kirsty had talked a lot, she took this to mean.

'And did she stay with you until you were all settled in here?'

'Yes, yes, of course.'

'And, Robert? Do you remember her fetching you from Station K.? Do you remember what happened down there?'

He waved his hand and rolled his eyes. She didn't know what he meant. If it was nothing, or it wasn't worth going over, or he didn't want to talk about all that now.

Someone appeared at the bedside and introduced himself as Dr Jones. He had a group of medical students with him. He had a lot of questions for Anna about the notes he'd been sent from Santiago. He wanted to know what the hospital had been like, and what procedures had or hadn't been done. Not everything was clear, he said. They'd be doing a new set of scans. He talked about physiotherapy and SLT, and support for a transfer home. He said he would be back in the morning.

Frank asked if they would be all right now. If he headed off. There was work, it was a work thing. Something had come up. He would be back as soon as. Anna mentioned that Robert had been looking forward to seeing him. Frank made an impatient noise, and said that he couldn't help it, something needed dealing with. He put one arm around her and told her to take care. She watched him walk away, his head bowed over his phone, and turned back to Robert. Robert rolled his eyes.

'Yes, yes, well obviously, yes.'

'All haste and no time,' Anna said. 'Isn't it? He'll be back. And Sara's coming up at the weekend.'

A woman with a tea trolley asked if they would like anything to drink. She gave Robert a menu for lunch and supper. The tea was poured into green china cups, with saucers. Anna waited for it to cool, and helped Robert lift the cup to his lips. He could hook one thumb into the handle, but he couldn't yet hold the cup straight. The tea trickled down through his beard, and she dabbed it away with her sleeve.

A bald man with a well-trimmed beard appeared beside the bed. He had broad shoulders and a pot belly. Anna recognised him from somewhere. He said his name was Michael, and he was from the Institute. More or less retired now. He was looking at Robert as he spoke, edging towards him, wiping his hands on his trousers.

'Doc. Bloody hell. Bit of a scrape.'

Robert looked at him and nodded. Anna remembered meeting him now, at a conference. He'd had a very loud laugh, and held the buffet plate too close to his mouth.

'My my my. My car.'

'Michael.'

'Yes, yes. Of course. My car.'

'They looking after you all right in here?'

'Yes, yes. Yes.'

'And, have they said? I mean, what's the—'

'Obviously.'

'The prognosis? Is this, I mean; recovery?'

He was turning to Anna as he spoke, losing confidence in Robert's ability to understand him, or respond. The doctors are saying we'll just have to wait and see, she said. Of course, of course, he nodded.

Robert waved a hand, and made a gesture towards the idea of getting out of bed.

'Wok, wok,' he said. 'Me, wok, mmm.'

He was looking for a word. He moved his hand over a series of small hurdles. Michael watched him carefully.

'Next, soon. In a little while?'

'Yes, yes.'

'You'll be back at work soon, Doc? Is that what you mean?'

'Yes, obviously. Soon.'

Michael turned to Anna, and raised his eyebrows.

'Robert? Robert, we'll have to see. Okay? We'll have to see.'

'Of course,' he said. 'Of course. Wok, wok.'

Another nurse came with the blood pressure monitor. Michael said he would leave them to it, and be back in a couple of days. The nurse fastened the cuff around Robert's arm, and pressed some buttons, and asked if he had any pains or discomfort. The machine beeped several times.

Anna stepped out into the corridor and checked her phone. There was a long voice message from Sara. She had been told her unfair dismissal claim was groundless. She hadn't paid any rent for two months, and her housemates had asked her to leave. She wanted to know if she could stay, just for a while, just until she got things sorted. Anna was appalled by how fiercely she wanted to say no. She said yes, of course. There was a text from Bridget, saying she would come over and cook dinner tonight and Anna wasn't to argue. Robert's sister wanted to come and stay. Her research director was hoping to catch up, just as soon as that was practical?

In the evening Bridget arrived with two shopping bags and went straight through to the kitchen. She pushed the hair out of her eyes and turned to Anna with her arms out.

'Come here, you idiot,' she said. Her embraces had always been longer and firmer than Anna was comfortable with, but they were never negotiable. Anna waited for this one to finish.

'I'm okay,' she said, before Bridget asked. 'I'm okay.'

'I know you are,' Bridget said. 'You always have been. So, listen, I'm doing something with tagliatelle. It involves a lot of cream. You good with that?'

She was already looking in Anna's cupboard for saucepans. She took a wine bottle out of her bag and waved it in Anna's direction.

'You want me to open that?' Anna asked.

'No,' Bridget said, 'I want you to stick it up your hole.'

Anna looked at her, and waited.

'Yes, Anna. I'd like you to open it. Thank you.'

Anna poured the wine and Bridget started chopping, talking about the trip she'd just been on and what trouble her children were in now, and about how she was thinking again of a career change, and once she had everything simmering away in a pan she wiped her hands on a tea towel and turned to Anna and said: 'But anyway, shut up now Bridget, how the fuck are you?'

It felt like the first time someone had asked this properly, and she didn't have an answer. People had offered to help, and asked what they could do, and asked how Robert was. She didn't know how she was.

'I'm behind with my work,' she said. 'I'm worried about Sara. I'm very tired.'

Bridget kept nodding, and Anna didn't know if that meant she knew these things, or she agreed, or she just wanted her to keep talking. She waited.

'I don't know if I want him to come home,' she said.

5 _

Someone had dressed Robert, and put him in the chair beside the bed. It was the first time she'd seen him in clothes since he'd left for Antarctica. It was the first time she'd seen him upright. He blinked at her quickly, opening and closing his mouth. Beds were for night-time now, a nurse told them. Robert had a lot of work to do.

'Yes, yes, well obviously of course, yes; wok, wok.'

He pulled at the collar of his shirt. Anna asked if it was uncomfortable.

'Yes! Yes! Obviously, Christ!'

'Okay. I was only asking.'

'Of course, of course, yes, yes.'

Bridget had wanted to know what she meant, about not wanting Robert to come home. Where else was he going to go? I don't know what I mean, Bridge. I just mean I don't think I'm ready. I've got a lot of work to do. They're going to have me filling out carer assessment forms. I don't want to be a carer; I never even really wanted to be a wife. Is it not a bit late for all that now, love?

Two physiotherapists appeared and introduced themselves. They weren't going to be Robert's friends, one of them said. It sounded like a joke but she looked serious. They were going to make him work hard. They pulled their chairs up close and ran through a series of tests. Turn your head from side to side. Drop your head to your chest. Lift your shoulders, and relax them again. Lift both arms as high as you can, and now hold them out to the side. Stretch your fingers out for me. Stretch them wider? Push back against my hand. Push back, really push back, Robert. Now the other hand? Anna took her laptop from the bag and tried to get on with some work. There were new deadlines she had to meet. Questions about methodology had been raised, and although they all knew the process had been robust, they needed to make that explicit. She looked up, and Robert was standing. The two physios were either side of him, and he was holding on to a walking frame, but he was standing by himself.

'Come on, Robert,' they said.

'I, I, can,' he said. 'Can, cunt!'

'He means *can't*,' Anna told them. Robert looked at her.

'Well, that's a relief,' one of the physios said.

'I – cunt – do,' Robert said. His whole body was trembling.

'You can't do it, I know. If you could do it, we wouldn't be here. But we want you to try. One step. Bend your knee. Let all your weight go into that standing foot. Yes.'

There was a voicemail from Brian at the Institute. He was back in Cambridge. He was sorry but they really needed to speak to Robert as part of their enquiries. There are certain details we need to put together, he said. I understand that communication is difficult, of course, but I wonder if there might be some way to facilitate this? If you could call me, please.

There were some texts from Sara but they were confusing. It wasn't clear if she was coming to stay or not.

Robert's sister wanted to visit.

All those years she'd resented him being away, she'd told Bridget. But they'd both got used to it. He's not ever going away now, is he? Let's deal with one thing at a time, Anna, love. You're still barely done reeling from the shock. There's a lot to think about. Let's get this bottle finished for a start.

The physios were still working. Robert was leaning forward slightly, the strain all over his body. He looked like he was leaning into a storm.

'Lift, bring it forward, down, down, let your weight settle, let your balance settle, keep your head up, okay, okay?'

His legs went out from under him all at once, and the two of them were right there to catch him. They eased him back into the chair so smoothly that it could have been their plan all along. Robert puffed out his cheeks, and widened his eyes, and avoided looking at Anna. The physios made notes, and said they wanted him to try again.

The woman came round with the tea trolley, and asked what they would like. Frank texted to say he was getting some legal advice. Robert slept, and Anna watched him, and she didn't know whether to hold his hand or slip away. She'd talked about their final argument again, and what she'd said, and Bridget had laughed briefly before making her face straight. Jesus, Anna, you make it sound like you laid down a curse. Well it's not something I feel good about saying. Sure, of course not, but this is not your fault, do you hear?

A nurse came and talked about medication. Someone else came and talked about diet. His blood pressure was checked, and his pulse. They were given leaflets about supported discharge, and people filled in forms. A man called William arrived, and said he was a speech and language therapist. He had some questions and he hoped to go through some exercises with Robert, if that was okay? He wanted to see where they were at, he said.

'Obviously, yes, of course,' Robert said. William found a chair and sat beside Robert and spread some picture tiles across a tray on his lap.

'Can you point to the picture of an aeroplane, Robert?'

Robert hesitated, and pointed. 'Pay-lane,' he said.

'Very good, Robert, yes. And can you point to something that floats?'

Robert lifted his hand. It hovered in the air.

'Something that floats, Robert? Floats on water? A boat? Can you see a boat?'

Robert waved his hand in front of his face. 'Christ,' he said. 'Yes, yes.' He looked at Anna, his eyes widening, asking for some kind of help. Anna looked over at the tray. There was a picture of a ship, with a row of windows and two funnels.

'I think William's asking you to point to the ship, Robert. There's no boat.'

'Yes, yes!' He rested a finger on the picture of the ship.

'That's right,' William said. 'A ship floats. A boat. Sorry, I didn't realise there was a difference.'

'Christ! Yes!'

'Right,' William said. 'Well. Can you point to something without an engine?'

Anna stood by the window and looked out at the car park. The cars were circling, looking for spaces. An ambulance tried to nudge its way between the solid lines of traffic.

'Something you pedal,' William prompted. 'We have a lot of them in Cambridge.'

Robert said nothing. Anna could see he was tiring.

'Okay, Robert; can you point to the bicycle?'

Robert nodded, and put his hand on the picture of the bike. William wrote something else on his form. Robert picked up the picture of a blue aeroplane, and turned to Anna.

'Red,' he said. 'Red, yes, well, obviously, of course. Red; here. Yes. Red – Christ!'

Anna looked at him. She had no idea what he was trying to say.

'Red, comb here. Mm. Mm. Christ! Brush, hair, head, mm, comb. Christ! Here, here, comb here. Okay okay, fucking, Christ, ha! Ha! Red, comb, here. Okay, okay. Oh, Christ!'

William leaned forward, and made a slowing-down gesture with his hands.

'Red. Yes. Red. Pay. Pay, pay, pain. Pain. Christ! Pain. Pay, lay, lay, lane. Ha! Pay lane.'

'Plane, Robert, yes. That's excellent; plane. But do you see the aeroplane in this picture is blue? Blue aeroplane. The car is red, here. Red car. Blue aeroplane. See?'

Robert pressed his hands against his thighs and straightened up, puffing his cheeks out in exasperation. 'Yes yes yes. Blue paylane yes. Christ. Obviously. Ha! Me, me, me. Eyes. Eyes. Eyes red paylane here, here. Phew! Christ! Red paylane bigger bigger here, phew!'

'Red car, Robert; blue plane. See?'

'Fucking fuck fuck yes! Yes! Fuck.'

William asked if Robert would like a break, and Anna said that perhaps he'd done enough for the day. She thought the frustration was keeping him from being able to concentrate, she said, and Robert turned to her, nodding. William suggested they could continue with something less pressured, but Robert was already closing his eyes to sleep.

–

At home she was woken late at night by Sara shouting at someone. She didn't know how long Sara had been there, or who else was in the house. She reached for the light and pulled on her dressing gown, and was halfway down the stairs before she realised no one was shouting back. By the time she got to the kitchen the argument was over, and Sara was glaring at her phone. Anna put the kettle on, and Sara told her not to say anything.

'I didn't,' Anna said, holding up her hands. 'I wasn't going to. It's nice to see you, by the way.'

'Don't.'

'I'm not going to. Tea?'

'Coffee, thanks.'

'At this time?'

'Mum?'

'Decaff?'

'Mum. Really?'

Anna boiled the kettle and made a coffee and a peppermint tea. She unloaded the dishwasher. They sat at the kitchen table together, blowing steam from the tops of their mugs. Neither of them knew what to say, or how to say it.

–

Someone had closed the curtains around Robert's bed. They could hear the encouraging voice of one of the nurses, and Robert's huffs and groans. Sara said *knock knock*, and ducked around the curtain, and Anna followed. Robert was getting dressed, sitting on the edge of the bed while he slowly worked the trousers up his legs. Sara sat on the bed beside him.

'Nice pants, Dad.'

'Yes, obviously, obviously.'

'Do you want a hand?'

Robert raised his eyebrows, and puffed out his cheeks. One of the nurses told Sara that they wanted Robert to do as much as possible without any help. She nodded, and shuffled away a little. Robert hooked his thumbs through the belt-loops of the trousers, working them up over his thighs. He shifted from one buttock to the other as he wriggled them up to his waist. The nurses made the occasional suggestion, and kept telling him how well he was doing. The trouser-fastening was two pop-studs, which he closed by slipping the palm of one hand underneath and pushing down with the heel of the other. When he had finished he was heaving for breath, but he lifted his fists above his head like a boxer, as if to say: look at me, I'm the damn champ.

Later, a woman called Laura arrived, and told them she was an occupational therapist. She talked about practical adaptations. Someone would come to the house for an assessment. Robert's mobility was improving but there might be a need for rails and suchlike. Was it a modern house? Sara made a snorting noise at this. Anna told her it was a comfortable house. Laura asked more questions, and filled in forms. She said she would arrange a home visit.

Sara did her best to make conversation, and Robert did his best to keep up. She had a lot to say about her personal life. He reached out for her hand and tried to squeeze it. She paused for breath and carried on.

Michael came back from the Institute. He hoped he wasn't interrupting. He hoped Robert was doing okay. He had brought some maps with him, and would it be okay if he looked at them with Doc? He spread one of the maps out across the wheeled meal-tray, and sat beside Robert to look over it. Here's the field hut. Here's Garrard Ridge. This is Priestley Head, at the edge of Lopez Sound. Robert was nodding. Yes, yes, obviously, yes, of course.

'And the medical team said they found you in this area, towards Priestley Head, within sight of the skiway?'

'Yes. Yes.'

'A tent was located here, beyond Priestley Head, along with a damaged skidoo.'

'Well, obviously.'

'Right. And Luke was found a few hundred yards beyond Priestley Head, disorientated but otherwise well.'

'Yes, yes.'

'Can you see, Doc? Over here?'

'Obviously, yes.'

'It's a long way from the field hut. It's a long way short of where Thomas was eventually recovered, at the far end of Lopez Sound.'

'Yes, yes. Ha! Yes.'

'I think, Doc, we're interested to know what they were doing over there. What Thomas was doing on the ice in the first place, and why they were travelling without satphones?'

135

'Yes.'

'Had there been any planning regarding the access onto the sea-ice? Any risk assessment?'

Robert widened his eyes suddenly, and made a puffing sound. He turned his hand in the air. The gesture could have meant: I don't know. Or: what can I tell you? Or even: these reckless young people! It was impossible to know. The three of them waited, and he did it again. Sara shifted towards him, and put a hand on his shoulder. Was this necessary, she wanted to know. Right now? Could this wait?

'Sorry, Doc. I know this is very difficult. This is an important point. Were you with Thomas when he went onto the ice?'

Robert turned to Anna. She caught something in his eyes. There was something he wanted her to say, or do. He turned back to Michael, and pointed at the map. He was pointing at Priestley Head.

'Here, here,' he said. Michael looked at him.

'Well, no,' he said. 'Thomas was found over here.' He tapped at the map, at the far shore of the Sound.

'Christ!' Robert shouted.

—

'Can you put your hand on the top of your head?'

Robert raised his eyebrows, and opened his mouth.

'The top of your head, Robert. Can you put your hand on your head?'

His eyes roamed around the room. It was striking to watch how literally he would search for an answer, sometimes. He lifted

136

his hands. He rubbed them across his face, slowly and firmly, as though he were washing.

'Head,' William said, softly, patting the top of his own head.

'Heh, heh, head,' Robert repeated. He moved his hands around the side of his head. He was watching for a reaction from William. He didn't touch his face again, but it was clear that he didn't know where to put his hands. He moved them around his head, waiting for a response. He rubbed his ears.

'Head,' William said, patting the top of his own head again.

'Heh – head,' Robert said, rubbing his temples.

'Now, can you touch your nose?'

There was a long pause while the information filtered through Robert's brain. The words had to take a longer way around now, as Anna understood it. She could measure their progress by the pace of his blinks. He didn't look to be in any hurry. William tried again.

'Your nose. Can you touch your nose?'

Robert looked down at himself. He looked at each arm in turn, and then back at William.

'Ha! Christ. Well.'

'Can you put a finger on your nose?'

Robert slowly brought his hand towards his face, and touched his nose.

'Very good. Nose. Can you say nose?'

'Christ, obviously. Nose. Nose.'

'Excellent. Great. Now then. Can you tell me the name for this?' William tapped his own shoulder, and then leaned forward and tapped Robert's. 'What do we call that?'

Robert moved his hand down to his own shoulder. His eyes widened, in understanding. His mouth opened and closed.

'Soul. Soul, soul. Jar. Soul, jar. Yes. Soul, jar. Obviously. Okay. Yes. Soul, jars. Well. Soldier, soldier.'

'Shoulder, Robert. Shoulder. Shh, shh, shoulder.'

'Shh, shh. Shh. Soldier. Yes yes. Soldier. Shhhhholdier.'

'Shoulder?'

—

They were just leaving for the day when Brian appeared on the ward. He said hello, and touched her elbow. It took her a moment to recognise him. It felt out of context. Santiago already felt like a long time ago.

'Brian, hello. This is my daughter, Sara.'

'Sara, pleased to meet you. And these are my colleagues: Michael, and Luke. I'm not sure if you've met Luke? He was at Station K., with Robert.'

There was a lot of handshaking. Anna watched Luke. He looked very young. He had a peculiar way of dipping his head each time he spoke. Hello, dip. Hello, nice to meet you, dip. Each time he dipped his head he adjusted his glasses. She turned back to the bed and saw that Robert was watching them. He had swivelled round on the bed and was trying to get to his feet. She walked towards him, and the others followed.

'Yes, yes. Hello. Hello. Obviously. Bye. Bye. Bye.'

'Brian. Hello. Good to see you again. I hear a rumour you'll be going home soon?'

'Yes, yes. Obviously of course yes.'

'I don't think that's been discussed yet,' Anna said.

Brian looked at her, and turned back to Robert. 'That's great. Great. And you'll remember Luke, of course.'

'Doc. Hey.'

Robert was standing now, leaning on the walking stick he had progressed to, and Luke stepped forward to shake his hand. Robert pulled Luke towards him, draping one arm around his back, and the two of them stood like that for a moment. Anna tried to remember if she had seen Robert embrace another man before. She wasn't sure that she had. As the two of them moved apart, she thought she heard Luke saying sorry, dipping his head. Sorry, Doc. Robert waved his hand in front of his face and clenched his lips: no, no. No need. He looked at everyone, and then looked beyond them to the ward entrance.

'And toe? Toe?'

'Robert?'

'Toe. Tom? Thomas?'

'Is he – he's asking where Thomas is.'

'Robert.'

'Thomas? Here?'

'Robert. Robert.'

'Here?'

6 _

Someone had taken Robert away. His bedcovers were rumpled and the sheets were still warm. His pyjamas were folded on the chair.

'Maybe he's gone to the pub,' Sara said.

'No, I don't think that's likely. It's rather early, and I'm not sure how he'd get there by himself.'

'Mum, I was joking?'

'Yes.'

They sat on the edge of his bed and waited. For some reason Sara reached across and held her hand. He'd probably been taken for a test, or a scan, or some physio. The impact of the stroke was being carefully assessed. His days were getting busier. It was important not to make assumptions about cognitive ability based on levels of communication. Stroke can have a significant impact on memory. She had had to tell Robert about Thomas's death all over again, once everyone had left. He could say *fuck* and *Christ* more clearly now, and the nurse-in-charge had come over to ask if he could please settle down.

On the way home Sara had got very upset, and asked how much better Robert would get. We're just going to have to wait and see, Anna told her. And was it his fault, do you think? Frank keeps talking about legal protection. Did he do something to mess up? Anna really didn't think so. He was always so thorough. He'd always told them that. All those years of experience. Sometimes accidents just happened. It didn't have to be anyone's fault.

The toilet door at the far end of the ward opened, and Robert appeared. His eyes looked wild. A nurse called over to ask if he was okay, and if he needed anyone to attend. He waved a hand in front of his face.

'Done,' he said. 'Done, yes, yes.'

He shuffled towards Anna and Sara, leaning to one side, propped up by the walking stick. They watched the concentration he brought to bear on simply not falling down.

'You managed everything by yourself then?' the nurse said, coming over. 'Excellent, well done!'

She put a hand on his shoulder, and with a slight flinch and a drop of his weight he shook it off. She smiled and went back to the desk. A look of disgust moved across his face as he glanced towards Anna and Sara.

'Christ, Christ. Me. Fucking. Me, med, medal! Me, medal.'

—

When she woke up she was in the chair beside Robert's bed. Robert was walking up and down the ward, his arm hooked through Sara's. Their heads were bowed together, and she was talking softly. When they got back to the bed Sara asked if she was okay. She told Anna she looked shattered, and Anna said she was just rather tired.

'Why don't you go home, Mum? I'll stay with Dad. You go and get some sleep.'

'But what if he needs something? What if they—?'

'We'll be all right, Mum. We'll cope, won't we, Dad?'

'Obviously, yes, yes. Of course. Yes.'

She told the nurse at the desk she was leaving. She checked that they had her phone number, in case she was needed. The nurse said she was sure her husband would be fine.

–

From the bus stop it was a twenty-minute walk to the house. The footpath ran narrowly along a flood embankment beside the river. There were willows with their feet in the water, young pollards sprouting from the stunted trunks. The river was high and brown, a white mist rolling over it. Figures appeared in the near distance, striding towards her, dogs running around their ankles or bounding up ahead.

At home she sat in the kitchen and waited for her heart to stop racing. Someone had put fresh milk in the fridge. There was work to do in the garden, and sheets to change on the beds. The laundry basket was full. She had shopping to do. The back door was jammed shut. The gutters were blocked. She didn't know how long Sara was planning to stay. She had missed two review meetings at work, and her head of department was leaving messages on the home phone. There were graphs to clean up, and presentation slides to work through. The Montreal Oceanography Conference IV was coming up and the team needed to be ready. Anna wanted to be able to play her part. She resented the time she'd lost. This should have been the high point of her career. Her research director had said it was difficult to know whether she should attend; she'd missed a lot of the legwork on the final stage, after all. Absolutely through no fault of her own, but they needed everyone to be completely up to speed. They all knew how quickly certain elements would jump on any mistakes. They'd both agreed to consider it carefully.

Two men arrived in a van. They were working on behalf of social services. They'd been given a list of home modifications. This was what Laura had promised. The occupational therapist. After her assessment. Anna didn't know they were coming today, she said, and they told her that wasn't unusual. Left hand don't know what the right hand's doing half the time, one of them said. She didn't understand what he meant. She let them in, and they worked their way around the house; attaching rails around the house, attaching rails and handles to the walls, a seat in the shower, and an arrangement of padded bars around the toilet. It made the house feel like a passenger ferry, with something to grab on to whenever the floor lurched and swayed. When they had finished, they were scrupulous about cleaning up after themselves. They drank tea, and told Anna what they'd done. They looked at their phones while they were talking to her, and talked about the next day's jobs between themselves, and when they left they wished her all the best.

There was a phone call from someone at the Cambridge meeting, asking how she was. They'd heard about Robert, he said. She opened and closed the back door a few times, trying to work out where it was sticking. It needed a good slam to get it closed. It would need taking down and planing. They had held Robert in their prayers, the man on the phone said. She didn't really know what he meant. She said thank you. She went out into the garden with the secateurs. She pruned the fruit trees and cut back the bushes, heaping the cuttings into a dead hedge beside the compost. The snowdrops had flowered. A robin followed her as she worked. She had been planning to go to meeting on Sunday, but now she wasn't sure. People would look at her. People would want to say, *And how are you?*

Strokes and seizures have been observed and sometimes treated in captive birds, but information on post-stroke recovery in wild birds is limited.

The sky darkened, the drains and ditches shining between the fields beyond the garden. She stretched. She wondered what Bridget was doing, and if she might want to come over for the evening. She stayed outside until it was too dark to see, and then she went down to the damson at the end of the garden and squatted over its roots. She'd pissed on the damson tree every year since they'd planted it, and still nobody knew. The steam rose all around her. She lifted her head, and watched the faint landing lights of airliners as they passed by overhead.

When she came back into the house her phone was buzzing on the kitchen table. There were several messages from Sara, telling her not to worry but that something had happened. It was Robert. Something had happened. He'd had a fall. Sara would try and call later, when there was more news.

—

Someone had called Frank, and he was waiting for her at the hospital in the morning when she arrived. She hardly thought that was necessary, especially when Sara had insisted she not come in last night. Robert had been briefly knocked unconscious when he'd fallen, but they'd taken him for a scan and found nothing wrong. Nothing more than was already wrong. Sara had stayed with him overnight, and now Frank was here as well. It was too much. He was waiting for her in the corridor. He wanted to talk to her before she'd had a chance to take off her coat or get a coffee.

'Why didn't you call me?'

'I didn't want to worry you. I thought you'd be too busy with work.'

They squeezed up against the wall while a porter pushed past with an empty bed.

'I'm worried already, Mum; this worries me, you know? This whole Dad's-had-a-stroke thing?'

'Okay.'

'You don't need to worry about not worrying me, Mum; just tell me about things when they happen, please?'

'Right. Okay.'

'We're not children any more. You can't do all this on your own.'

'Okay.'

He made a sound that was halfway between a sigh and a groan, and raised his hands in the air. She looked at him.

'Why do you? Why do you get like that?'

'Like what?'

'Like, all shut down, monosyllabic.' He flattened his voice, and muttered: 'Okay, right, yes, okay.'

'Is that; are you doing an impression of me? I don't know what you mean, Frank.'

'You do, Mum, you really do. It's like you pull down the shutters.'

'Well, I don't know what you want me to say; I'm not disagreeing with you.'

'Anything, Mum, anything more than just *okay*.'

'You do realise that *okay* is not actually a monosyllable?'

He made the noise again, and turned away. Another porter came past, pushing a woman in a wheelchair. She waved at them both as she passed, regally.

On the ward, Dr Jones was waiting to talk to them. There were messages on her phone from Robert's sister, from Brian at the Institute, from a parcel delivery company, and from her colleagues at work. She had nothing in for dinner that night. The house desperately needed cleaning. She needed to find time to get to the office. Dr Jones said Robert's fall hadn't caused any damage, and that the brain's natural plasticity should continue to produce improvements in language and mobility. The Supported Discharge Team would do a full assessment, but Robert should be home in a few days. He was medically well enough. He no longer required hospital care. Dr Jones knew it would be a challenge for them all, but patients almost always recovered more successfully when they were cared for in the community. She questioned his use of the word *community*. There was only her at home, she reminded him. She couldn't be a community by herself. The Supported Discharge Team would ensure a package of measures was in place, he told her, and asked if she had any other questions.

A nurse came and checked Robert's blood pressure. William was running through some exercises with the patient in the next bed along. The physios were asking the young man opposite to put a finger on his nose, and he was looking at them as if he expected further clarification. There was an empty lunch tray on Robert's bedside locker. The nurse asked Robert if he had any pain or discomfort, and Robert said, yes, yes, obviously yes. Christ! He waved a hand in front of his face. It was a gesture that looked like he wanted to wipe the slate clean: no, that's not it. That's not it at all.

–

Someone had packed Robert's bag when she got there in the morning, and emptied his locker. Someone had brought him a wheelchair, and now he was sitting in it at the end of the ward. One of the cleaners was busy around his bed. The nurse-in-charge came over and told Robert that it had been lovely having him but he was to try not to come back. He waved his hand in front of his face to say *no*. Anna asked if they should just leave, and the nurse-in-charge said that no, of course not, transport had been arranged.

They waited. She texted Sara and Frank to say they were waiting for transport. They both replied to wish her luck and say they would try and come up again soon. Give Dad my love. Hope he's doing okay. She asked Robert if he was okay. He looked at her and puffed out his cheeks, widening his eyes. He did this a lot now. It seemed to mean something like: well, this is big, that's a big question, this is a lot to ask.

Eventually two drivers came and found them, and wheeled Robert outside. They used a ramp to get him up into the ambulance, and again to get him out once they'd arrived at the house. Anna told them both times that in fact he could walk a few steps, but they just said they had their instructions. They also insisted on using a special carry-chair to get him up the stairs. Their manner when they discussed how to do this didn't fill Anna with confidence.

'Could you just sit him in the front room, and we'll worry about the stairs later?'

'No, no it's fine love, don't worry. We've been told to get him up to the bedroom. He'll be fine. Don't worry, Mr Wright. We're well trained. Just hang on tight.'

'Yes, yes. Obviously. Christ!'

Once they'd got him into bed they stood for a moment while they both got their breath back. She had to sign some forms. It was like signing for a package. I have inspected the merchandise and it was delivered in an undamaged condition. They thumped down the stairs and let themselves out. She looked down at Robert and he closed his eyes. Sleep came to him so quickly now. She took all the boxes of medication and arranged them on the dressing table. She would need to make a chart of what he was taking and when. She looked around the room, listening to him breathe.

In the evening she cooked pasta. She had to keep going back upstairs to check on him. He was asleep. When she'd drained the pasta she stirred in some olives and some hard cheese. It wasn't much of a homecoming meal but she didn't want to leave him on his own. She carried two plates of it up on a tray, and ate hers while she waited for him to wake up. She helped him to eat, and then she helped him to wipe his face, and then she helped him to the bathroom. Everything took a long time. He was almost asleep when he got back into bed, and she told him to shout if he needed anything. Before going to bed she sat in the kitchen with the lights turned off, looking out at the garden and the fenland beyond. There was a glow of electric light around the horizon. There was a roaring sound in her ears. She had the same dizzy sensation she sometimes got at the end of a long train journey. She felt ill-equipped, despite the preparations that had been made. She had questions she couldn't quite articulate. She sat and listened for any noises upstairs. She waited for the spinning to subside.

7 _

She had to change the bedsheets in the morning because he'd
made a mess of using the pan. She had to help him roll out of the
bed and lever himself into the chair. She had to put a towel on
the armchair because his pyjamas were still wet. She had to get
him out of the wet pyjamas and wash him down with a soaped
flannel and a bowl of hot water. She had to get him dry and into
warm clothes before his temperature dropped. She had to get
down on her knees to put the socks on his feet, and his feet into
the trousers. She had to cajole him into pulling the trousers up
by himself; hooking his thumbs into the belt-loops, wriggling
them up from side to side. She had to help. She had to ignore,
for the moment, what he was trying to tell her. She had to
concentrate on getting the job done, on keeping him warm. She
had to get some food into him before his blood sugar dropped
too low. She had to leave him in the armchair while she went
down to the kitchen, and she had to make him promise not to
move. She had to listen out for any crashes or noises while she
sliced an apple, and spread toast, and made tea. She had to ignore
the phone while she ran the breakfast tray upstairs. She had to
cut the toast into small pieces so he could eat it. She had to count

out his tablets while he was eating, and tick them off. She had to carefully take the mug away from him when she heard him call out, and wipe the hot tea from his hand and his clothes. She had to tell him again to let her help him with hot drinks. She had to ignore the angry expression on his face. She had to bring him the tablets and watch him swallow them. She had to open the windows to air the room. She had to ignore the phone because he needed to go to the toilet. She had to help him stand slowly, and walk with him along the landing, and help him to lower his trousers and sit on the loo. She had to give him his privacy, and wait outside the door. She had to change the bedsheets, still, as soon as she got the chance.

She had to answer the door while Robert was in the toilet. Whoever it was had already knocked twice. She told him not to move and ran down the stairs, and a woman called Cathy held up her ID. She was with HomeCare Services, she would be working with Robert Wright, they would have told Anna about this at the hospital? She came in with a bag and a thick bundle of paperwork, and Anna said she had to run back upstairs. Cathy came with her, saying you'll not mind I'll come with you, and when Anna went in to Robert the conversation carried on through the bathroom door.

'I'll be coming three times in the week now,' she told them. 'General check-up and personal care and anything else that needs doing.' Robert looked frantic. Anna tried to explain but Cathy was still talking. She checked Robert's date of birth and middle name, and asked if any issues had arisen. Anna helped Robert to clean himself, and wash his hands, and then she opened the bathroom door.

'It's a pleasure to meet you, Mr Wright,' Cathy said. Robert held out his hand.

'Yes, obviously. Of course.'

She walked with him back to the bedroom. She asked what he'd been eating, and talked about *spending pennies* and *number twos*. She undressed him and checked him all over for pressure sores. She told them what each of her own children did for a living, and about the grandchildren she had to collect from school. She told them how many appointments she had that day, and how her car was *on its last legs*. She thanked Robert for putting up with her, and she carried her bag down the stairs. She told Anna thank you but she couldn't stop for a cup of tea.

'I'll see you on Wednesday,' she said, as she got into her car. 'God willing. Same sort of time.'

—

She had to return a call from the speech and language service, and confirm the first home visit. She had to contact someone at the Institute, and talk to them about Robert's sick pay. She had to apply for an extension on her compassionate leave. She had to talk to somebody at the Institute about arranging a visit for Robert, who was desperate to get to the office and see people. He was under the impression that he would soon be returning to work. She had to find a way of discussing how difficult this might be. She had to reply to Luke Adebayo, who had asked if he could visit. She had to let Robert's sister know when she could come and stay, and reply to a string of other text messages asking for news. She had to pull out the dishwasher and unblock the drainage hose. She had to wash the laundry again because she'd left it sitting too long in the machine. When she made dinner she had to cook the onions in margarine because there was no oil and she couldn't get to the shops. She had to carry the dinner up to Robert on a tray, and cut up his food, and sit with him while he ate. She had to air the room, again.

She had to look at her emails and messages in the evenings, once Robert was settled. There was a long email from her research director, with several attachments, detailing their plans for the Montreal conference. This was all just for information now. She wasn't being asked for input. She was just being *kept in the loop*. There were emails from several campaign groups she was subscribed to, with urgent actions that would only take a minute of her time. There was an email from Brian at the Institute, talking about the inquest for Thomas Myers and saying they would need to look at the best way of including Robert's account. When she heard Robert shuffling to the bathroom upstairs she had to sit very still and listen until he was safely back in bed.

By the end of the week she had to ask Sara to come and help, just for a while. It was too much. She didn't think she could do it all on her own. She resented having to say this aloud. She went out into the garden to make the phone call, to make sure Robert wouldn't hear.

'It doesn't need to be for long,' she said. 'I just need a chance to get things straight.' She could hear Sara hesitating. It was a clear day and the sun was warm on her face. There was a plane banking gently way overhead, coming in on the Stansted approach. The buds on the damson were starting to open. The new rhubarb was already a foot tall. The beds and borders needed weeding. The raspberry canes needed tying in. Robert had been asleep when she came outside, but she didn't want to leave him for too long. He'd been trying to do things by himself when she wasn't there. She needed to start thinking about lunch. Sara was asking when she'd last seen Frank.

'The thing is, Mum, I've just started this new job. I don't know if they'll give me the time off. I'd really like to help. But. Is there someone you can call? In the meantime? Have they told you anything about home help?'

She had to bring chairs into the bedroom and make it present-able, for when people came to visit. A lot of people came to visit. Don't go to any trouble, they all said, before telling her how many sugars they took. Michael and Brian came from the Institute, with a woman from the speech therapy service. There were things they needed to clear up, they said, and they were hoping the woman could help present their questions to Robert. Her name was Liz, she said. She was due to start working with Robert shortly in any case. This was a funny way to meet him first. She wasn't a trained advocate, she told Brian. If this moved to a legal context they would need to appoint a specialist. She could only advise them on a very limited basis?

They had brought another map of Station K., and were using coins to represent Robert, Thomas, and Luke. The three of them clustered together, at the edge of the Sound. They talked about the storm, and showed Thomas drifting across Lopez Sound.

'Sand. Leaf full sand. Huh. Loaf full sand.'

'Lopez Sound?'

'Of course, of course.'

They asked about radio communication. They asked about what had happened with the skidoo.

'There were no radio communications with the main base at this point,' Michael said. 'We're still trying to confirm why this was. Luke has said that Doc's behaviour became erratic.'

'Erratic?'

'He thought alcohol was a factor. But obviously we don't know when Doc's stroke occurred. That may have played a part. His decision-making may have been inhibited.'

'Doc, can you show us where the skidoo accident took place?'

Robert looked at each of them, and at the map. Liz found a picture of a skidoo on her phone, and moved her hand across the map.

'Skidoo. Crash?' She clapped her hands together when she said *crash*. Robert nodded. 'Crash? Where? Here?'

He circled his hand somewhere around the foot of Priestley Head.

'Here,' he said. Michael nodded.

'Okay. And Luke got you into a tent, and went on to find Thomas?'

'Obviously, yes. Strict structures. Christ! Or, order.' He waved his hand.

'Robert,' Liz asked, 'are you saying you *ordered* Luke? Strict instructions?'

'Yes! Of course!'

'You gave him strict instructions to go and find Thomas?'

Robert waved his hand again, vigorously.

'Strict instructions *not* to go and find Thomas?'

'Of course, of course! Too too long, long, too *late*. Safe safe. Strict structures.'

'So, Robert. You told Luke *not* to go and look for Thomas? It was too late? Safer to stay in the tent?'

'Yes, yes.'

'And he went against your advice? Continued on to look for Thomas?'

'Obviously, obviously.'

'And did you have any further contact with him, or with Thomas, by radio?'

'Yes.' He waved a hand in front of his face.

'He means no. He's saying no.'

'Doc, did you see either Luke or Thomas after that?'

He waved the hand: no, no I can't. He looked up at the ceiling. He looked at Anna. Anna asked if they could come back the next day. He's still in the very early stages of recovery, she told them. He's tiring very quickly. He needs more time. He was already closing his eyes.

She had to find him things to do, constantly. He had a short attention span, but no tolerance for being unoccupied. Frank had given him an iPad loaded with speech therapy apps, and although he still needed her help getting started, he seemed to enjoy working through those. She became familiar with the Midwestern American accent of the woman on the app. *Put these words in the correct category: tulip, daffodil, daisy. Flowers is the correct answer. Hammer, screwdriver, wrench. Tools is the correct answer.* The sound of the woman's voice drifted down from upstairs, with Robert tutting and swearing as he tried to jab at the screen. *Repeat these useful phrases. Help me.* Hemp, hemp. *I'm thirsty.* Fussy, fussing, fuss me. *Good morning.* Good again. Good again. *Can you speak slowly, please.* Yes! Christ! Spen, so. So. Christ. Spen. *Please speak slowly.*

She had to get the washing out on the line while the weather was clear. She had to ignore all the jobs she wanted to do out there. She had to run in from the garden and let Cathy in, when she finally heard the knocking.

'I was starting to think you had me down as one of those cold-callers,' Cathy said, lugging her bag through the door and straight up the stairs. 'Not to worry, not to worry, I'll be straight up and see to him. How's he been, how have you been, lovey? Where is he? In the bedroom still? Afternoon, Mr Wright, how are you doing? Still in your pyjamas?'

'Yes, yes, of course.'

Robert was in bed, looking through a stack of his old sketchbooks and journals. He'd gone to a lot of trouble to ask Anna for them, and she'd had to go into the loft to track them down.

'We can't be having that. Healthy young man like you? Lying around in your bed all day? You'll give yourself a bad heart.'

'Sleep sleep. Tired.'

'Well, you will be tired if you stay in bed. Stands to reason. Okay, let's have a look at you.'

She pulled his pyjama top over his head and lifted the waistband of his trousers, checking for sores. She washed her hands and sorted through his medications. She asked if he had any pain or discomfort. She said if it was any of her business it was high time they got this lazybones down those stairs. At the front door Anna tried to tell Cathy that Robert was experiencing low moods, that she couldn't talk him into getting up and getting dressed, but

Cathy said no matter how difficult it was, it had to be done. His mood's only going to get lower stuck in that bed, she said, scribbling something on her paperwork as she walked back to her car and saying she'd be back again in a few days from now. She never looked at her watch, but she was always out of the house within fourteen minutes.

She had to carry Robert's dinner up on a tray, and sit with him while he ate. She had to air the room. She had to look at her emails and messages in the evenings, once Robert was settled. She had to drink coffee to stay awake. She had to sit very still and listen when she heard Robert moving around upstairs. And when she heard a muffled thump from the bathroom, she had to run up there and break down the door. She was surprised by how easily the lock tore through the frame. She would have to repair it. He was lying on the floor beside the toilet, wedged in against the wall. His trousers were around his ankles and she couldn't move him. There was a long smear of shit down the back of his legs, and vomit on his face. She asked if he could push himself up from the floor, and he howled. She grabbed a towel and wiped at his face, scared of him choking. She tried dragging him across the floor but he was too heavy. She had to run for her phone and call Bridget, saying she was sorry it was so late but she needed help, and Bridget said she would be there as soon as she could. While she waited, she tried to get Robert clean; wiping between his legs with a warm flannel and towelling him dry, cleaning his face and hair and beard with more flannels, rinsing out his mouth with cold water. She put a pillow under his head and a blanket over him. It took a long time to work the vomit out of his beard. When she was done she sat beside him on the bathroom floor, wedged in between the toilet and the sink, holding his hand and stroking his head. He squeezed her hand a few times, and hummed loudly, and fell asleep.

8 —

She had to make Robert learn to use the stairs, Bridget insisted. You can't let him spend the rest of his life in the bedroom. The physios said he was ready to be home. You've just got to push him a bit more. Anna flung open the curtains and told him what a fine morning it was. The sun was already high and she was planning to work in the garden. She'd put out a blanket on the bench. Didn't he want to come and sit outside?

He looked at her and shrugged. He had reason not to answer her now, when he didn't want to.

'Hard. Hard hard. Legs. Hard.'

'I know. I know it's hard. All this is hard. The physios said you had to keep moving. You have to keep pushing.'

'Cunt.'

'I know it feels like you can't, but.'

He was waving a hand in front of his face, which was still as close as he could get to shaking his head or saying no.

'Cunt,' he said, again. She looked at him, and he held her gaze. He was breathing quickly.

'Robert. I'm not going to argue. I don't want us to argue. But I've made some lunch and I'm not going to carry it upstairs.'

She turned around and left the room. She went into the bathroom and splashed her face with cold water and screamed into a folded towel.

When she came back into the bedroom he held up his arms, and she helped him lever himself out of the chair. At the top of the stairs she had her own doubts. It suddenly looked a long way down. She wouldn't be able to catch him if he fell. He held on to the handrail with both hands. He slid one foot to the edge of the first step. She leaned forward and guided it over the edge, and down. He shifted his weight to that foot, then slid his other foot down to join it.

'There we go. There we go. You can do this, Robert.'

He was already breathing heavily. He slid his foot over the next step.

—

I have difficulty speaking, but I can understand you. I have difficulty. I have hard, hard. *I have difficulty speaking.* I have hard speaking. *But I can understand you.* I am hard speaking but I can stand. Stand you.

—

The new speech therapist came back for his first proper session. Liz. She had a quiet voice but she spoke very clearly. She was older than the speech therapist at the hospital, and seemed more relaxed. She talked about the notes she'd received from her colleagues, and said that she didn't want to go over old ground. She was keen to work with Robert on what she called *communication strategies*. Ways you can work around your language barriers, she said. She mimed someone climbing around or over a wall as she said this, and Robert nodded. She did a lot of miming, and encouraged Robert to do the same. His heart didn't seem to be in it.

They were sitting at the kitchen table. She had folders of notes and learning materials. Anna was making drinks. Liz said she wanted to start by setting some benchmarks.

'Is that okay with you, Robert?'

'Yes, yes, of course.'

'Thank you, Robert. Okay, so. We have some yes and no questions first of all; I know you've been having difficulty with *no*, so could you hold your hand up if you want to say no? Can we try that?'

'Yes, yes, of course.'

'Is your name Robert?'

'Yes, yes.'

'Is your name Peter?'

Robert held up his hand, nodding.

'Okay. Now then. Does breakfast come before lunch?'

'Yes, yes, obviously.'

'Does a car hold more people than a bus?'

Again, Robert held up his hand.

'Can you fit ten wedding rings in a shoebox?'

'Ha! Christ. Ten! Ten! So, so, yes. Yes.'

'Great, thank you Robert, okay. Now, I'm going to say three words that I want you to remember. Don't worry if you can't say them properly.'

'Christ!'

'Okay, hang on. Three words, listen: walk, sun, red. Can you say those?'

'Christ! Yes, yes. Wok. Wok. Ssss, song. Red. Christ!'

'That's great, Robert: walk, sun, red. Okay. Remember those words and I'll ask you again in a moment. Can you tell me how many days are in a week?'

Robert looked at her for a moment, nodding.

'Days,' he said. 'Days.' He tapped his fingers against his leg, counting off the days. 'Sen,' he said, holding up five fingers. 'Sen? Sedden. Sedden. Christ!'

'Are you saying seven, Robert?'

'Yes, yes, obviously. Sedden.'

'You're holding up five fingers there.'

Robert looked at his hand, and looked at Liz. 'Yes, yes. Sedden.'

'Okay, thank you. And can you tell me how many suits there are in a deck of cards?'

'Yes, yes.'

'Playing cards? There are hearts, and clubs; those are suits. How many suits are there?'

'Far! Christ, yes. Foo, are, four. Four.'

'Four? Yes, that's great. Four suits in a deck of cards. Okay. And can you tell me the three words I asked you to remember just now?'

Robert looked at her, and at Anna.

'Yes, yes, obviously, of course. Christ!'

He waited. Liz waited.

'Three words, Robert? The first one was walk?'

'Wok, wok. Yes, yes, obviously.'

Liz prompted him for all three of the words, and Robert just about managed to repeat them. They ran through some more exercises, and then Liz talked about how limited the resources available to community speech and language services were, and about the range of apps and self-guided therapy exercises he might be able to take on. Anna wasn't sure if she was talking to her or to Robert.

—

She had to get Robert settled on the bench with a blanket over his legs before she could do any work in the garden. The blossom was out. The freshness of it took her by surprise, again. The bright whites and yellows and pinks. The energy of it. He made a big show of smelling the air, making snorting noises and puffing out his cheeks.

'Sing, sing sing. Fuck. Christ. Sing.'

'You're going to sing for us now?'

He waved a hand in front of his face. No. No. He waved a hand at the garden. Something about this.

'Try again.'

'Sing. Win ter. Sing.'

'Spring?'

'Yes! Obviously. Yes. Sing! Fuck.'

'Spring. Yes it is. It's definitely spring.'

He puffed again, pleased at having made himself understood. She knelt on the edge of the grass and made a start on the weeds.

—

Make these shapes with your mouth: puh, buh, muh, duh, suh.

—

Cathy's visits came to an end after three weeks.

'You'll miss me now, won't you, Mr Wright?' Cathy sorted through her paperwork, and made some notes. She asked Robert to strip so she could examine him. Robert began unbuttoning his shirt. He was still only using one hand.

'It gets worse every year,' Cathy said. 'It does. Five, ten years ago, I'd have been in here every day. And there'd have been two of me. Two of me, Mr Wright! You'd have liked that. Now it's desperate. It's priorities. You've got Mrs Wright here at home with you, so there's less danger. You've got family who come and help out. You score zero, you know? I've got those on my list who are on their own, no family, no neighbours checking in. I call round and they're in the same chair I left them in. Even some of those I'm down to every other day, and I'm with them thirty minutes at most before I've to scoot off to the next one. It gets so I'm not sure I even want to do the job, only I can't be sure anyone would want to do it in my place, you know? For this money? I'm not complaining. The money's never been great. But I'm doing twice the work for the same pay I was getting five years ago. But listen to me now. Tell me to shut up, will you? The upshot is you're on your own, I'm afraid. I warned you not to get too cosy with me, didn't I? Now, if you can arrange for your wife to abandon you, that'd be a different lookout altogether. Poor old Mr Wright all on his lonesome? They'd have me back in no time. What would you think about that now?'

After fourteen minutes she was in the car and driving down the road. It had rained overnight. There was mud on the road. The fields were thickening with the early shoots of barley and rye.

—

She had to get him ready for another visit from Liz. He woke up in an awful mood, growling and sullen, and refused to get out of bed. Even with the weakness down his right side he was still stronger than she was, and she was never going to force him out of bed.

'Robert, you know Liz is coming today. Don't you want to show her all the progress you've made? All the work you've been doing with the app?'

'Can't. Can't. Tom, tom, tom. Day. Nex day.'

'Tomorrow? She can't come tomorrow, Robert. She's coming today. You're going to have to get up. Come on. I need to change these sheets anyway.'

'Tom, tom. Nex day. Sleep. Sleep.'

'Robert, you can't go back to sleep now. Come on. Don't make life any harder for me, please. Get dressed and we'll have some breakfast, okay?'

'Sleep!'

'Right. I'm making some coffee. Yours will be downstairs. Get yourself dressed.'

'No!'

She was halfway down the stairs before she realised what he'd said. She went back up.

'What did you say?'

'No!'

He heard himself, and his eyes widened in surprise. He nodded.

'No, no. No!'

'Well, there now. That's going to make life a bit easier. Didn't Liz say that words would just start coming back by themselves?'

'No, no, no, no, no.'

'Well, she did.'

'Yes, yes, obviously.'

'Of course.'

'No, no, no, no, no, no, no.'

'All right, there's no need to overdo it.'

'No.'

'I'm making a coffee, do you want one?'

'No. Yes! Yes. Yes.'

'It'll be waiting for you downstairs. When you're dressed.'

'No. Yes!'

—

She had to put clean sheets on the spare-room bed, when Sara turned up unexpectedly. Sara was sorry she hadn't been able to come in the week. The new job was hectic and she couldn't get the time.

'But let me know what I can do while I'm here,' she said, calling up the stairs. Anna wrestled with the bedding. The clean duvet cover had gone on inside out, and she left it. She scooped up her clothes from the chair and the floor, and carried them through to Robert's room. Their room. She sat on the bed. All the pillows were gathered into the middle, where he'd been sleeping.

She didn't want Sara to know she'd still been in the spare room, for some reason. She didn't know how she felt about sharing Robert's bed. They had been wary around each other since he'd been home. She was spending so much time helping him dress, helping him wash, helping him backwards and forwards to the toilet. It was difficult to see past that and think about him as her husband, her partner, a man she had once wanted to kiss.

She opened the windows to air the room, and stripped the sheets from the bed. She carried all the bedding down to the washing machine, and asked Sara to put the kettle on.

In the morning Sara appeared at their door with two mugs of tea. Anna had been awake for a while, listening to Robert's steady breathing and feeling the warmth of his body beside her. She had been trying not to think about what would happen next. She sat up in bed and propped the pillows behind her and took one of the mugs of tea. Robert shifted his body from side to side. Sara opened the curtains, and sat at the end of the bed. Robert worked his way up to a sitting position. Anna helped him to arrange the pillows. They sat with their mugs of tea, waiting for them to cool, while Sara looked on.

'What – she – wants? Want mon, mon. Cash. Want, cash?'

Sara laughed.

'Dad, you're dead right. You're very perceptive. I'm in desperate need of a loan, so I've made you a cup of tea to soften you up. You've got me.'

'Yes yes, obviously of course. I – knows you. Knows you – when.' He held out a hand to the side of the bed, showing how tall she'd been when she'd first come climbing into their bed by herself. Sara laughed. Anna was watching her.

'Are you serious? Do you really need money?'

'Mum! No! It was a joke, I was joking; I told you, I've got a new job, it's going well.'

Robert asked, haltingly, what the new job was, and Sara said something opaque about digital marketing strategies. Anna started to ask more about it, but then Robert made the noise he made when he needed the toilet, and by the time she'd got him out of bed and standing up it was too late.

—

Put these words into the correct category: water, tea, wine. Sandwiches is the wrong answer. Water, tea, wine. Drinks is the correct answer. I am thirsty, I would like a drink. Fuss, fuss. Drink.

—

She had to get the bedding out on the line and dried before evening. It was good to be outside. The leaves were full out on the fruit trees and the hedges. The grass was thickening a deeper green. She would leave it to grow tall and set seed. Beyond the garden the farmers were spraying again. She had to get the baked potatoes in the oven. She had to tidy the living room, and make sure Robert had rested. Luke was coming to visit.

—

Robert already had the maps out on the dining table when Luke arrived. He had traced three coloured lines around the map of Station K. A red line showing Thomas drifting along the Sound; blue and green lines showing Luke and Robert travelling from the field hut and across the end of the skiway; the beginnings of a green line moving away from the scene of the skidoo accident. The lines wavered, uncertainly.

When Luke rang the doorbell, Anna didn't know how to respond. She couldn't show him in and stand next to Robert at the same time. She hovered halfway between the two. Sara looked at her oddly and went to open the door. Luke remembered her name from the hospital, and said hello. He took off his shoes in the hall, and waited to be invited in. Robert was sitting at the far side of the dining table, and when Sara brought Luke through, he kept his face lowered over the maps. Luke edged towards him. Robert looked up.

'You all right then, Doc?'

'Lu, lu, lu. Lu. Luka.'

Luke nodded, and tried to hold Robert's gaze.

'Yeah, Luke. It's been a while. How's it going?'

'Well.'

'Yeah.'

'Obviously.'

'Yeah.'

'Of course.'

The two of them looked at each other, properly. Luke was wiping his hands down the sides of his trousers. Anna was aware of standing too close. She said she would put the kettle on, and moved away out of the room. From the kitchen she heard Sara

170

trying to start a conversation. She asked Luke what it had been like working with Robert. She asked if he would be going back to Antarctica again for the next season. It didn't sound like she was giving Robert much chance to speak.

When Anna came back into the room, Luke was sitting at the table with Robert and looking at the map. He was talking about the mapping projects the team was working on at the moment, and about their plans for the coming year. Robert was leaning forward, and squinting in the way he did when he really wanted to listen.

'They're going to put a satellite link in, Doc.'

'Well, yes. Obviously. Obviously.'

'Wi-fi at Station K. YouTube all evening. No more charades.'

'Ha! Christ.'

Anna handed out the teas, and asked Luke how he was feeling about going back to Station K, after what had happened. Sara looked at her suddenly, with a sharpness she couldn't interpret.

'Yeah. Weird, I guess. My mum's not happy. I've promised her I'll stay close to the hut. But I reckon you have to get back on the horse, don't you?'

'On the horse?'

'Yeah, I mean, you know; get back to it. Before it gets too big a deal.'

'Right. Yes. Of course. On the horse. You went straight back to the Peninsula that time, didn't you, Robert? After what happened to Tim?'

'Yes, yes. Of course, yes.'

Robert turned his face to the window. Luke asked if he'd been in touch with anyone on the team. Robert didn't hear him, perhaps. Luke waited, and asked him again.

'A few of his colleagues have been in to see Robert, yes. He's been keen to get back to things. He was hoping to be involved in the training conference. But there are some challenges.'

'Right, yeah. I bet you miss it though, eh, Doc?'

Robert didn't say anything. Everyone waited. Luke was looking out at the garden, looking at Robert, working out what to say next. Anna could hear Robert's breathing deepen. Sara had moved away to the sofa, and was watching Luke.

Robert tapped on the table suddenly. He circled his hand over the map, and then flung it up into the air, making his puffing sound.

'Go, go. Gone,' he said.

'You can't remember what happened,' Anna said. 'It's gone?'

'Yes, yes, obviously, obviously.'

'I don't know what I can tell you,' Luke said. 'Some of it was confusing, you know?'

'Of course. Yes.'

'I didn't know what was happening with you.'

'Huh, huh. Yes.'

'We didn't know where Thomas was, if he was going to make landfall or not.'

'Long. Long full sound.'

'Lopez Sound, right.'

'Yes, yes.'

'I stayed with you for a long time, Doc. Like, two hours, in that storm. You were out of it. You'd said it was too risky to go after Thomas. I mean, it was hard to understand what you were saying, but I got that.

'Yes, yes. Yes. Yes!'

'So I waited. I thought help was on the way. I thought they'd be there. Any minute. But I couldn't. You know. I couldn't stand being stuck in that tent while Thomas was. You know.'

'Yes, yes. Gone.'

'Right. But maybe not gone. We didn't know. So I left you. I thought I could get to him. I thought you'd be safe. The weather was brutal but I thought you'd be safe in the tent at least.'

'Sub, sub. Stub.'

'Stubborn? Yeah, I guess.'

'Order.'

'Well, it wasn't an order though. It was advice. By the time I got going, the wind had dropped but I couldn't see far. There was more climbing than I expected, to get round the back of Priestley Head and get to the shore. It didn't feel safe. I kept trying Thomas on the radio but there was no response. When the weather cleared completely and the plane came in, I could just about still see the tent. And I could see you, way off, going back to the skiway.'

'Well, yes. Obviously. Good. Good.'

'I tried, Doc.'

'Yes! Yes!'

'I tried to bring him back.'

'Obviously. Good.'

'It was too.'

'Yes. Yes.'

'I saw the plane come in. I got on the radio as soon as I saw them. Told them to look for Thomas. Because the flare had gone up, the emergency flare.'

'Christ. What? Yes. Pay-lane. Red pay-lane. Yes.'

'Did you see the flare, Doc? Way past Priestley Head?'

Sara had stood up, suddenly, and was walking towards the table. Robert turned to look at her. Something was happening that Anna didn't understand.

'Red pay-lane. Small, small.'

'You saw the plane.'

'Small, small. Come bigger.'

'He was still, you know. He sent the flare up?'

Robert screwed up his face suddenly, and waved a hand over the map. He looked to Anna for help of some sort. Sara got to him first.

'I'm sorry, Luke. Dad gets tired very quickly at the moment.'

'Of course, yeah, sorry. Sorry.'

'No, don't apologise. It's fine. It's really good of you to come. Dad's been looking forward to seeing you, haven't you?'

'Yes. Yes. Obviously. Yes.'

'It's just, it's difficult for him to concentrate for very long.'

'Sure. Yeah. Sorry. I'll make a move.'

As he stood up he tapped the map, and Robert looked at him. Sara walked with him out to his car, and through the window Anna watched them talking. Robert was making the noise he made when he needed the toilet, and she had to help him out of the chair.

–

Press your lips together. Open your mouth wide. Repeat these sounds:
fah, fah, fah. Sah, sah, sah. Mah, mah, mah.

—

The next morning after breakfast Sara said she was taking Robert for a walk. Robert didn't look as though he'd been consulted.

'I'm not sure that's a great idea,' Anna said. 'I'm not sure how far you'll get.' Robert was already up and looking for his coat.

'Mum, I'm not stupid. We won't go far. I'll be careful. But he needs to start getting out and about, doesn't he?'

There were thumping sounds coming from the coat cupboard in the hall. Robert came back, holding his boots.

'Sun – day, walk. Pub!'

'Well, you might not get as far as the pub. See how you go. Will you be careful?'

Robert bowed his head, solemnly.

'Yes yes, obviously of course. Care. Care.'

Sara knelt down and helped him on with his boots.

'Take your phone. Don't go far. Call me. Be sensible.'

The two of them waved at her over their shoulders. Neither of them turned around. Sara was holding Robert's arm, and already sounded more talkative than she'd been all weekend. They turned onto the footpath that ran behind the house, and Anna closed the door. She put on her boots and went out into the back garden. The phone in the hallway rang and she ignored it. She stood between the damson trees at the end of the garden and watched the two of them make their slow stately progress along the raised footpath beside the drainage dyke. It was almost impossible to see

175

Robert's limp. Sara was doing a nice job of matching his pace. They looked as though they were taking their time by choice. Their heads were bowed slightly together, and Anna wanted to know what they were saying. She wanted one of them to turn and wave. The sun was high and the earth smelled ripe and new. The leaves were bright and thin on the trees and the light shone through them as they moved in the wind, and just as she was settling down into the silence her phone started ringing and Sara said, Mum, I'm sorry, it's Dad.

9 _

She had to listen to Frank talk about the inquest, several times.
Sara had told him about Luke's visit. Frank said she should ask
the Institute to provide legal support. She should make sure he
had his own solicitor. Anna told him that Robert wasn't on trial;
no one was on trial. The inquest was a formality, to confirm how
Thomas had died. It wasn't an investigation. No one was going to
blame Robert, surely?

She had to put Frank on speakerphone so he could tell Robert
not to say sorry. An apology would be an admission of guilt, he
said.

'But what if he does feel sorry? I feel sorry that the boy died.
We all do. I'm sure Robert does. What's he going to say when he
sees the boy's parents?'

'Mum, he can't say he's sorry. Whatever he says, he can't say
that. Do you hear me, Dad? No *sorry*, okay?

'Ha! Yes. Obviously. So. So, so. Sorry.'

'No, Dad. No sorry.'

'Obviously. Obviously.'

—

Can you repeat that. Can you re, re, repeat. *I don't understand.* I no stand. Not stand. *I don't understand.* I do stand. Do understand. *I don't understand. Can you speak more slowly please.*

—

She had to get Robert ready for Liz, and she had to tidy the front room.

They were working on real-life situations. Liz had gathered that they didn't have a car, and relied on the bus to get into town, so she wanted Robert to practise catching the bus by himself. Anna found it hard to picture him catching the bus by himself. Liz arranged the dining chairs into two rows, and sat at the front.

'I'm the driver,' she told Robert. 'You step onto the bus.' Robert nodded, and stepped towards Liz. He looked at her. He was waiting for her to ask a question.

'The driver won't ask where you want to go. You have to speak first. Okay?'

Robert looked round at Anna. He seemed confused by what he was being asked to do. Anna stepped in front of him.

'Single to the city centre please,' she said.

'Two pound fifty,' Liz said, handing over an imaginary ticket. Anna took her seat at the back of the bus, and watched Robert step forward.

'Sin, sin. Sing. Sin gull. Sin gull. Sin, sin. Sing. Sin gull. Sin gull. Sen sen, settee, sen.'

'So, you might get stuck on the place name, okay? So there might be a route map you can point to, somewhere in the bus? Or you could bring a bus timetable with you, and point to your desti-

178

nation there? Or write it down first? There are lots of ways of working around the problem, do you see? With some planning?'

Robert was nodding. He stepped backwards, and then mimed stepping onto the bus again.

'Sin gull,' he said, pointing to a piece of imagined paper in his hand.

'Very good. Great. Then I'll tell you the correct fare, and you put the money down, and we're on the move.'

Robert turned to Anna, beaming, as though he'd passed a great test. She tried to imagine him ever actually going out on his own; catching buses, walking into shops, asking for directions. He really didn't seem ready for that.

'Robert? Will you take a seat so I can drive on?'

—

Open your mouth wide. Stretch. Hold for three seconds. Relax. Press your top lip over your bottom lip. Hold. Relax. Touch the left corner of your lips with the tip of your tongue. Hold. Touch the right corner of your lips with the tip of your tongue. Hold. Relax.

—

She had to get up when she saw the first light through the curtains. She had barely slept. She eased out of bed and went to the window. The fields and ditches were shining wetly. The horizon was edged with orange and red. She dressed quickly and made a mug of tea and carried it outside. Robert would sleep for another hour or so. He wouldn't notice she'd been gone. She followed the footpath past the side of the house, towards the river. The footpath was slick with mud and she stepped carefully, sipping at the hot tea as it sloshed over the edge of the mug. Swallows flashed across the meadow on the other side of the drainage ditch, and a long line of heavy-winged geese sloped by above her. When she got to the river she crouched at the edge of the flood embankment and watched the water churn down towards the sea. Her breath spilled into the air. Vapour trails stretched overhead, tying the bright horizon to the navy-blue night in the west. Downstream the road bridge throbbed with red lights. She looked down the embankment, picturing the river climbing higher and higher until it spread across the fields and houses behind her. Picturing all those cars trying to drive through the floodwater regardless. Heading to the airports, the commuter villages, the customer collection points. She finished her tea. She threw the mug into the water and watched it sink. She had to get back to the house.

—

She had to lock herself in the bathroom sometimes, just for the privacy. He had become more mobile, and had lost confidence. He followed her around the house like a child. He moved so slowly and quietly that it was often a surprise to turn and see him there. He'd made her jump, several times. She didn't know if he wanted the company, or if he was just bored. He seemed pleased with himself for getting around so much. When she came out of the bathroom sometimes he was just standing there, waiting.

'Robert. Were you there the whole time?'

'Yes, yes, obviously.'

'Well, you want to watch that. You'll get yourself in trouble, listening outside bathroom doors like that. I could have been doing anything in there.'

'No, no, no, no.'

'You know I'll be back in a minute, okay?'

'Wait. Waiting. Yes, yes. Waiting.'

'Fine, but you don't need to wait right outside the door.'

'Yes, yes.'

–

She had to slow down, according to Bridget. She couldn't do everything she was trying to do without breaking herself, she said, on the phone. Had she thought about taking a year out from work altogether? Anna explained how important the Montreal conference was, how it would feed into the next IPCC; how much time her team had spent fine-tuning the models and cleaning the data. Bridget listened, and asked if Anna thought they might be able to solve climate change without her, just about? Anna paused. She needed to strip the bed. This is one of those *tongue-in-cheek* questions, isn't it? she asked. It is, Bridget said. But you take my point? Anna kept the phone crooked between her shoulder and ear while she untangled the duvet cover from the duvet. Will you think about it, chicken? Anna looked up at the ceiling. This is what I do, she whispered. This is all I do. She could hear Bridget nodding. She carried the bedding downstairs. There was no time to stop. Bridget was saying something else. She had to empty the dishwasher. Robert was safely in the garden, with a book about mountain rescue open in his lap. It wasn't clear how much he could read but he liked to turn the pages. Bridget wanted to know how they were doing, how the two of them were doing.

Through the kitchen window Anna could see the shadows lengthen along the road. The crows were circling and settling into the thin strip of woodland on the far side of the field. Robert would be getting cold out there in the garden, even with the blanket on his knees.

'Honestly, Bridget, I don't know. I don't know. There's so much. I mean. Isn't there?'

She held up a glass to the light. It was streaked with sandy smears. The filter needed cleaning again. Bridget waited.

'I used to think about. I was; I had thought about. You know. Considering my options. Is that? I did. But now. No. It doesn't. It wouldn't be. What would. No. You know what this is now. You know what this means. I should have. Years ago. Years. I could. But now. Not now. No.'

Robert was standing behind her, waiting to put his empty mug beside the sink. A look passed between them. Bridget's voice came from the other end of the phone, asking Anna if she was still there. Robert moved through to the front room, one arm held out for balance, ready to catch his fall.

—

She had to get the house ready for everyone coming up for the inquest. Frank would be there, and Sara, and Robert's sister and her husband, and Bridget of course. They couldn't all stay at the house but they would all be passing through. There was food to prepare, and tables to clear, and Bridget brought some folding chairs over in the back of her car.

She had to help Robert dress for the occasion. He could just about manage his shirt buttons but the tie was beyond him. She didn't find it that easy herself. It took a few minutes. When it was done, she rested her hands on his chest and leaned against him. The rustle of their breathing was a comfort. There was a kiss. Everyone was waiting downstairs.

When they got there Anna realised she'd been expecting a court, but the ushers showed them into something more like a conference room. She was surprised not to see a flip chart. They sat in rows, facing a heavy oak table at the front, and when the Coroner came in someone asked them to stand.

People took it in turns to go to the witness table and explain what they knew about Thomas's death. The people from the Institute kept using acronyms, and the Coroner kept asking them to clarify. This is a matter of public record, she said, and I'd like the public to understand. I'd like Thomas's family to understand.

Thomas's parents were sitting in the front row. There was a young woman with them. Anna didn't know if this was a sister, or girlfriend, or someone else. She was short and slim, and she watched everything with a steady concentration. When she shifted in her chair Anna could see the muscles moving in her shoulders.

When Luke was called he looked nervous. He was asked why Thomas had gone onto the ice, and how it was they had become separated during the storm. He said that Thomas only stepped on the ice briefly to take photographs. He said that the storm started very suddenly, and that he'd become disorientated. He and Robert had been in close proximity to Thomas when the storm began, he said.

When Sara heard this she made a soft wincing sound, as though she'd pulled a muscle. Anna turned to ask her what was wrong, and Sara shook her head.

He was asked if he had made any attempt to contact Bluff Point, from the field hut. I asked Doc to, he said. I believe an attempt was made.

When it was Robert's turn, the advocate went and stood alongside him, and began by explaining his communication deficits. His memory of the time around the incident is extremely limited, he told the Coroner. It's also possible that as a result of the stroke his cognition was limited. The Coroner asked several questions, and a map was displayed on a big screen. He was asked if he'd heard any radio communications, once Luke had left him in the tent, or whether he'd seen the blue smoke of an emergency flare. No, he said. Obviously, obviously. No. Thomas's family had brought a solicitor, who said he had further questions.

'There were two daily scheduled radio communications with the main base at Bluff Point?'

'Yes, of course. Yes.'

'And these took place at nine a.m. and six p.m., every day?'

'Obviously, of course. Yes.'

'And a failure to respond to those scheduled communications would trigger a search and rescue response, correct?'

'Yes.'

'Which is what ultimately happened, as we know.'

'Yes.'

'And you are allowed to contact the main base at other times, in case of any difficulties?'

'Of course, of course.'

'But when you discovered that Thomas was adrift on the ice floe, and you set out with Luke to rescue him, you didn't contact the main base?'

Robert looked at the solicitor. He looked at the advocate beside him. He looked out at the rows of people watching him. The advocate asked him something. Robert's eyes were roaming. The solicitor waited.

'Ray, ray. Radio.'

'Could you rephrase that question, please? Do you want to know if Robert contacted the base?'

'Sorry, yes. Mr Wright: we know the satellite phones had lost power due to poor battery maintenance. Did you use the High Frequency radio to contact the main base at Bluff Point?'

'Ray, ray. Radio. Obviously. Radio.'

'Because there is no record of any contact from you.'

'I. Ah. Yes, yes.'

'Mr Wright. Why didn't you contact the main base, and request assistance?'

'I. Ah. Sorry. Sorry. No. No. Christ.'

'Mr Wright?'

The advocate said something to Robert, very slowly. Robert lowered his head to listen. Beside her, Anna could see Frank clenching his fists, and screwing up his eyes.

'Ah. See. See. Bow, bow. Row. Bow – roke. Broken.' He was making a snapping gesture with his hands.

'The radio was broken, you're saying?'

'Yes. Yes. Obviously, yes. Bow. Broken.'

'Okay. Can we check, sorry: do you mean *broken* as in physically damaged, permanently, or *broken* as in not functioning adequately at that moment?'

The advocate looked at the solicitor for a long moment.

'Could we have a go at rephrasing that question, do you think?'

–

She had to cook for everyone in the evening. Bridget came back with her to help. She came into the kitchen with a list of what everyone wanted to drink, and said she didn't know if it felt like a wake or a birthday or a what in there. Nobody wanted to admit they were celebrating, she said.

'Well, it's a relief at least,' Anna suggested.

'Would you say so?'

'Frank would.'

'I'm sure. Listen, get those glasses down.'

–

Liz told them about a new support group that Robert had been invited to join. It was aimed at people who were moving into the next stages of their recovery process, and would no longer be receiving one-to-one speech and language therapy.

'No longer be receiving?'

'No. This was always a limited intervention, I'm afraid. Our resources are – stretched.'

'Christ! Ha!'

'This is it? He's finished?'

'Not at all, no. Robert's language will keep developing, we hope. He can keep up the self-guided work. I'll check in from time to time. And this group will be very helpful.'

'Wok, wok. Obviously. Wok.'

He wanted to go back to work. He wanted the speech therapy to have fixed everything, and it wasn't going to. He was used to working with things that could be repaired or replaced. Liz talked about how much progress he could continue to make, and about the other communication strategies they'd discussed. The group wasn't a speech therapy group, she said, but everyone there would have communication difficulties and would be working to develop their communication. She would be involved in the group, but it would mainly be run by a lovely young woman called Amira. She had some really interesting ideas, and she'd managed to secure some generous funding.

—

She had to talk him into it, over several days.

She had to plan their route carefully, and allow plenty of time. She said she wanted him to buy his own bus ticket, and he looked as though anything else would have been absurd. She had to find the right change. She had to kneel down and tie his shoelaces.

They walked out from the house, and down beside the river. The footpath on the flood embankment was hard and cracked. The water level was low. He had brought his stick but was trying not to use it. There was a sharp puff of breath with every other step, but she knew not to ask if he was okay.

It took forty-five minutes to walk to the village, and by the time he was sitting at the bus stop his face was flushed and sweating. She uncapped a bottle of water from her bag and offered it to him. The street was empty and quiet, and the heat rose from the tarmac. The forecast was for rain and thunder. She had packed umbrellas.

The meeting room was in a university health centre building, near a park. She had to ask two different people at the reception desk where they needed to go. When they got into the lift Robert started shaking his head.

'No, no, no. Not. No.'

'Robert?'

'No. No. Christ! No.'

'What's wrong, Robert?'

The lift doors opened and they stepped out. He waved his hand up and down the corridor, meaning: this, all this is no good.

'Well, we've come this far. We might as well go in and have a look.'

'No. No, no.'

'You don't have to come again if you don't like it. But, really – we went to a lot of trouble to get here, didn't we? Sorry. Really.'

'Ha!' He was amused by something. His mood shifted. He set off down the corridor the wrong way. She had to fetch him back. There was some confusion about where the room was. When they found it, a woman was waiting outside, with a clipboard. Robert peered past her, into the room.

'Hi, hello, hello. My name's Amira. You're here for the group?'

Robert watched her. Anna said that yes, Robert was here for the group. Robert Wright.

'And you'll be Anna? Anna Wright?'

Somebody was waiting behind them, in a wheelchair. Robert made a big show of moving out of the way. The woman in the wheelchair nodded her thanks, and a young man pushed her in through the door. Amira gave her a name badge as she passed, and then told Robert and Anna they were welcome to come through. Anna could see a small circle of chairs in the middle of the room. Liz was there, sitting at the far end of the room, next to a trolley with a coffee machine and a plate of biscuits. She looked up, and waved. Amira was offering Robert a name badge. Robert was shaking his head again.

Anna was suddenly very tired.

STAND |

1 |

'Look at your. Everyone? Good morning. Can we just. Let's make a start. Okay? Can we? I want to begin by asking. Okay? I want you all to just look at your hands. Are we ready?'

They weren't ready. They weren't even all sitting down in the chairs she had so carefully arranged in a circle. One lady kept standing up and pushing her chair to a slightly different angle. There was a gentleman talking very loudly about football to the lady in the wheelchair beside him. The lady in the wheelchair was looking at him sceptically, saying nothing. There was another gentleman over by the coffee machine, trying to balance a cup and saucer in one hand while leaning heavily on a stick. Several people were struggling with their name badges. Amira decided to just keep talking, in the hope they would gradually settle.

'Okay. Those of you who are ready? We're going to start with a little exercise. I want you to let your hands sit loosely in your lap, if you can. Palms up. Close together. Okay? If we can all take our seats now. There'll be a chance for questions in a moment. I just. I was hoping we could settle with this exercise first. So. Hands. Yes. Hands in our laps, palms up. Like this. Supporters as well. That's right. If we could all. Yes. If we could all come and sit down now?'

|

Anna watched her trying to gather the group's attention. She had told them her name was Amira, writing it in large looping letters on a whiteboard beside her, and again on a name badge. Her voice was soft. She waited until everyone was doing as she asked, looking around the circle at each person in turn, smiling. The room quietened. Anna was distracted by noises in the corridor: a conversation moving past the door, a trolley with a squeaking wheel. Traffic on the busy road outside. Robert shifted in his seat beside her, and dropped his hands into his lap with a grunt.

'Lovely,' Amira said. 'Thank you. So. Look at your hands.' She was young. She sat slightly forward in her chair, with her back very straight. Her hair was pulled away from her face, and fixed into a neat French braid. 'Look at the shape of them. Look at the way they sit in your lap. Are they flat? Are they curled? Are they the same as each other? Really the same?'

The room was a good size, but crowded. There was a lot of equipment pushed up against the walls – running machines and exercise bikes, flip charts, wheeled whiteboards, catering trolleys – and the space felt cluttered. But there were those tall windows at the end of the room, looking out through a row of trees to a park and the river beyond, and once people had settled into their chairs all that light helped the room to feel calm.

There were a dozen of them in the circle, men and women, mostly older than Robert. It was difficult to tell who was a patient and who was a carer, except that some people in the circle seemed less inclined to speak. *Patient* was the wrong word, she suspected. *Carer* was almost right.

'Look at all the different elements that make up what we call a hand,' Amira said. 'Look. The wrist, the palm, the thumb and fingers, the joints, the knuckles, the tendons. See?'

There was a siren in the street outside. Robert turned to look, and Anna watched him looking. His head was trembling a little, in a way that had become familiar. As though the weight of his skull were too much for his neck to bear. He had an expression on his face that made it look as though he'd eaten something unpleasant.

|

Liz kept an eye on each member of the group as Amira ran through the opening exercise. They had gone over it together but this was the first time Amira had tried it for real. It was already starting to feel a bit wordy.

'Well, but! This hand, bloody useless! See, see, bloody useless see?'

Pauline was lifting up her limp right hand with her left, and shaking it around. Liz had warned Amira, when they were planning the sessions, that Pauline would be quick to ask questions.

'Yes, yes, I do see that. Hello – Pauline? Yes. Many of us here will have limited use of one hand, or even both hands. I'll be coming on to that. And it's difficult. I know it must be—'

'Useless! Don't want, I don't want to look at it, see?'

'No, and that's fine. That's fair enough. Nothing we do here in the group is going to be compulsory, I should say that right at the beginning. If there's anything you're not comfortable with.'

Pauline stood up again to rearrange her chair. She was tall, and very thin, and was having trouble finding a comfortable sitting position. Her skin was deeply lined in a way that Liz suspected came from too much smoking, or sunbathing, or both. She was in her late fifties, and two years on from her stroke. Her sister was with her. Carol. She was younger, and looked tired whenever Liz saw her. Carol spoke quietly to Pauline now, and Pauline nodded.

'On, on. Carry on,' Pauline said, waving her hand in a gesture of permission.

'Thank you, Pauline.' Amira paused, letting the room settle again. 'Okay. Is everyone still with me? I just; I just want us to all really look at our hands. Look at the skin. The lines in the skin. The calluses, the blisters, the scratches and scars. Our hands tell a story, don't they?'

|

There were no scratches or scars on Amira's hands, Anna noticed. They were immaculate. This exercise was designed to be relaxing, she supposed. To put people at ease. Anna didn't feel either of those things. She felt impatient, and resentful, and just really very tired. Pauline stood up again to adjust her chair, and Carol eased her back into her seat.

Amira was talking about visualisation, and telling them to breathe. Breathe. Breathe.

'Oh yes, true! Very good. Yes, that's right.'

196

The man with *Raymond* on his name badge was holding his hands up to the people around him, showing them something. His wife, Barbara, was tutting and telling him to hush again.

'Is that? Is there something, Raymond, is there something you'd like to show us?'

'Oh, yes, very good. Very good. That's right.'

Raymond held up both hands. There was a pale pink scar running across the palms of both hands, vivid against his skin. A chatter of horrified approval went around the group.

'Wow, Raymond, that's quite a scar. That's. Is that new? Is there a story behind it? Do you feel comfortable sharing it with us?'

'Oh, yes, yes. Very good. Trick trick. Trickity, that's right, yes. Trickity. Pzzzz! Ha! Pzzzz! That's right!'

'Somebody played a trick on you, Raymond?'

'Umm, well now, trick, trick, trickity. Pzzzz! That's right.'

He held up his hands and gripped hold of an imaginary bar. As his grip closed around it, his eyes suddenly widened and his whole body shook. Robert jolted in surprise beside Anna.

'Trickity, yes!'

'Electricity,' Barbara explained. 'My husband was an electrician, you know. He had an accident at work. On a building site. Long time ago. He likes telling the story still though now. Yes he does.'

'Well, Raymond,' Amira said, sympathetically. 'That must have been quite a shock.'

|

She didn't realise what she'd said until it was too late. The laughter was loud and hectic. People called out what she'd said, or they tried to, and Raymond repeated his mime of grabbing hold of the live wire. Amira watched everyone for a few moments. She needed to let these outbursts run their course. The lady in the wheelchair, Mary, was saying nothing, but she was taking an interest and nodding along to something. The bearded man, Robert, had folded his arms, and was gripping his name badge in one fist. Viktor was watching impassively. Raymond was apologising to his wife, and shaking his head, and smiling to himself. Pauline was sighing heavily, and looking out of the window. It had started raining outside, and the light in the room dimmed a little.

'Okay. Thank you, Raymond. We'll be hearing all sorts of stories from each other as we go through these meetings, I hope. I'm looking forward to that. Thank you. Okay, everyone? So. We're looking at our hands. And I know that some of us have no movement in one hand, or very little. So just do what you can with this exercise. Look at the shape of your hands, as they rest in your lap. You'll see that, resting, they form a natural cup shape. Can you see that? Imagine how comfortably something could sit in your hands, right now. Try to imagine the weight of it, okay?'

|

Liz watched Amira fetch a box from a shelf beside the door. She could see that things were moving too quickly for most of the group. You wouldn't even call them a group, yet. Liz was only there to monitor, and to offer practical help when needed, and she didn't want to tread on Amira's toes. But it would be worth talking through in the follow-up.

Amira moved around the circle, placing a foam ball from the box into each person's hand. She didn't want them to do anything with it yet, she explained. Just let it rest there. When she came to Pauline, she crouched in front of her and said something softly. Pauline turned from the window and looked at her. Even with half the muscles in Pauline's face failing, Liz could see the disdain. It was in the eyes, mostly. Her sister reached over and pressed the red foam ball into Pauline's right hand, levering her thumb across it to keep it in place. With a grunt of effort, Pauline pulled her hand away.

'Don't think about holding the ball just yet,' Amira said, once she'd handed them all out. 'Let it rest in your hand. Try to feel the touch of it. The texture. The pressure. Okay? Remember: when we think about thinking, we are learning how to think. Your brain is making new pathways, new connections.'

She was standing in front of her chair now, leaning her weight forwards and keeping her body language open. She was very careful about enunciating her words, Liz noted. This was helpful. Her drama training, probably. The way she insisted on making eye contact with everyone in the room.

'I'll ask your supporters to now just gently roll that ball around in the cup of your hand, pushing against each of your fingers.'

|

Supporters. This was a new one to Anna. It was usually *carers,* or occasionally *partners. Supporter* was more neutral, perhaps. It included the people here who looked like nursing staff, rather than family. Like the young man who had pushed Mary into the room in her wheelchair, and was now sitting beside her, or the young woman sitting with a distracted-looking man in a suit.

'Now, watch each finger as the weight of the ball pushes it down into your lap. Feel that movement. Feel the pull of each tendon along your finger and the back of your hand, and up into your—'

'Can't do it! No, no!' Pauline had dropped her ball on the floor, and was complaining loudly.

'Oh, yes, that's right; very good, very good,' said Raymond.

Amira stepped forward, into the centre of the circle, and paused. She picked up Pauline's ball, and held it. She said something about not everyone finding this easy, and taking things at different paces. Robert was restless in the chair beside her. He was squeezing the ball tightly, and banging his hand against his leg. She watched him.

'Now. Not all of you will be able to do this today. That's fine. That's good. That's part of the journey we're on together. Relax for a moment. Breathe. Breathe. Breathe.'

Anna felt something shift in the quality of Robert's attention. The trembling in his head softened. His breathing quickened a little. He stood up, in a way that Anna imagined was meant to be abrupt but in fact took some time.

'Christ! Yes, yes. Of course. Right! Of course.'

'Robert, are you?' Amira watched him. 'Do you need to take a break?'

'Oh, yes, that's right! Very good, very good.' Raymond's wife put a hand on his arm and tried to still him. She was looking at Anna. They were all looking at her. They wanted her to stop Robert, perhaps? To make him sit down? He was already on his way to the door. Anna watched him. She picked up her bag and coat, and Robert's coat, and told Amira she was sorry. Amira stood, smiling, and tried to touch her arm.

'It's fine, it's fine. I understand how difficult things can be. I hope we'll see you both next week? Perhaps we can have a chat about how to make things easier for Robert?' Her face was close to Anna's. She was talking quietly, as though this were a secret. Anna nodded, and said okay, and followed Robert. He was waiting at the door. He couldn't open it. She piled everything onto one arm and held the door for him. He didn't look at her. He muttered his way down the corridor. As Anna closed the door she saw everyone in the circle looking at her, their hands in their laps, the light coming through the tall windows, and the expressions on all those faces. She didn't know how they would be able to go back.

2 |

Viktor was the first to arrive, the next week. He looked as though he'd made sure of it. He was out of breath as he pushed open the door, and he stumbled a little. Liz put out her arm to support him.

'Is early? Is okay?'

'Hi, no, it's fine, Viktor, you're not early. Come in, come in. Can you find your name badge here?'

'Yes. Is not.' He sighed. He looked at the badges, laid out on the table beside the door, and tapped at the first letter. Amira leaned in to look at it.

'Sorry, is the name wrong? Have I spelled *Viktor* wrong? I took all the names from the referral letters, but somebody could have made a mistake?'

'No. Yes. Is Wiktor. Same. Okay. Is. Ahh.' He was trying to draw the shape of the letters in the air with his finger. Liz could see the problem now.

'That's not how you spell it,' she said. 'Sorry, that's probably my fault.'

'Let me get you a new one,' Amira said. 'I've got some spares. Can you write it?'

Wiktor peered at her over the top of his glasses: yes, he could write, he was saying.

'This, good. Viktor, Wiktor, okay. Same sound. Spelling. Small thing. Sorry. My speak. I.'

'Oh, I see, yes. Got it. Wiktor. That's fine, fine, no need to apologise, really.'

'My. Okay. My British. Nnngg. Speak British.'

'Your English?'

'Yes, yes, okay, my English. Was good. Perfect. Now. Is gone.'

'That must be very difficult for you, Wiktor.'

Wiktor's accent had developed after his stroke. It had taken several sessions to establish this, and it was only once he showed her a video of himself that Liz had really understood. The video was of him speaking at an IT conference, about networking nodes. She hadn't understood all of it, although he had been speaking perfectly clearly. In the video he'd had a faint north London accent, and a well-projected voice, and the only sign of nerves had been in the way he kept taking his glasses off to look at his notes and then putting them back on again.

'Wiktor's parents came here from Poland before he even started school,' she explained to Amira. 'He didn't have this accent before his stroke. You do struggle with the way your voice sounds now, don't you, Wiktor? Is that fair to say?'

'Yes. Hard. Hard. Sound, like. Like. Foreign, okay? No, no, no. Not this.'

'You're not a foreigner. No. I understand.' Amira smiled, again. He held the badge, with his name spelled correctly. He held it to his chest and looked at her. She took it from him, and pinned it to his shirt.

'There.'

'Yes. Thank. Thank. Okay.'

|

Amira hadn't known whether anyone would come back. The first meeting hadn't really been a success. She'd discussed this with Liz. She had jumped into the first exercise too quickly. Liz had suggested that today they could spend time going over the aims of the group, and establishing some ground rules. She suggested seating everyone around a table, so that resources could be passed around. Amira wanted to get them up and moving, but Liz said it was a bit soon for that. Let's get them comfortable as a group first, she said. Let's develop their trust. They opened out three trestle tables, and arranged the chairs around them. It looked like a boardroom. Amira wanted to suggest something else, but then Wiktor arrived and there was no time to change it.

Mary arrived soon afterwards, her care worker backing through the door and reversing her into the room. She was wearing a tweed trouser suit and a large wooden necklace, and there was something about the way she held one hand near her face that made Amira think she would rather be outside, smoking. She collected her badge from the table, and her care worker wheeled her into place before taking himself off to the corner to look at his phone.

There was a flurry of arrivals then, and Amira noticed people passing name badges to each other. Recognising each other already. *Sean. Pauline. Carol. Raymond. Robert.* Robert didn't speak to anybody, and didn't wear his badge. But he was there. Amira said hello to his wife, Anna, who nodded quickly without actually meeting her eye.

|

The leaves on the trees outside had started to fall, and more light was coming in through the windows. They were plane trees, with the bark sloughed off in patches. It was a clear day. There were two young children in the park, and dog walkers down by the river. The traffic was slow on the road. Anna kept her face to the window while people moved around the tables and settled into their seats. It was taking them a while. There was a lot of broken conversation, and people changing their mind about where to sit. Even Robert was shifting around in the seat beside her. He wouldn't wear his name badge yet. She wasn't sure why he'd agreed to come at all. His curiosity about life outside the house was enough, perhaps.

Amira had called her during the week. She said she wanted to *check in*. Anna had told her this was all very new for Robert, still, and there was a lot he was unhappy about. Amira understood that. Anna had asked questions about the group's purpose, Amira's remit, the funding stream, the proposed outcomes. She'd been struck by Amira's willingness to answer her questions.

I don't know about Robert, she'd told Bridget, but it's a relief to be around other people who can't. You know. Can't always find their words.

And are they all as annoying as Robert? Bridget had asked. Anna didn't think this was fair. It was the wrong word. *Difficult* might be more like it. *Exhausting.* His frustration at not being able to speak kept tipping over into frustration with her for not understanding. He would get angry, and then remorseful, and then sentimental. There was a lot of crying. She didn't always have the time.

I don't think so, she'd said.

Give it time, Bridget had said, laughing. Wait, Anna had wanted to say. Wait, it's not like that. It's not like that at all. But Bridget had already moved on to something else.

Amira started talking. Anna turned away from the window, shifted her chair a little closer to Robert's, and listened.

|

It took a few moments for everyone to settle. Amira looked around the table and waited. She welcomed them all back, and started to talk about what the group was for.

'We didn't really discuss this last week,' she acknowledged. 'I think we all got a bit distracted. So: the first thing to say is that we're not here to do speech therapy. I'm not a speech therapist. You've done that work with Liz. And of course that will carry on in various ways. What we are here for is to think about our communication strategies. There are lots of ways of communicating that aren't just about speech. I'm sure we all use lots of them already.' She picked up a stack of laminated cards.

'And mostly we're here to have fun, okay? Just to get you out of the house once in a while?'

'Oh! That's right,' said Raymond, loudly. 'Very true, very good. That's right.'

206

Amira nodded in acknowledgement. It was important to acknowledge, but also to keep things moving. Raymond nodded back and turned to his wife, looking pleased with himself.

'So. Each week, just to kind of check in, I'd like us all to introduce ourselves, and tell each other how we're feeling now, and how our week has been.' She held up the first card, showing them a row of emoji faces in different colours. 'Okay? You can use the pictures here, see? Happy face, sad face, angry face.' She pointed to the last face in the row: a blue face with raised eyebrows and a wobbling mouth. 'What's this one here, do we think?'

'Don't want to!'

'You think so, Pauline? Okay, this is the don't-want-to face, for if that's how you're feeling. I'm sure we all know that feeling. Okay? Okay, I'll start. My name is Amira, and today I am feeling, this one: the worried face.' She held up another laminated card, with a series of clip-art illustrations of people engaged in various activities. 'My week has been, this one: this person sitting at a computer, busy with work, that's me. Okay. Can I give you these, Pauline?'

Pauline took the laminated cards, and stood up to rearrange her chair. She sat down and looked at the cards, turning them over in her hands.

'Right. Pauline. Happy.'

'Happy? I thought you said you were feeling don't-want-to?'

'No. No! Happy.'

'Okay, great. And this week? What's your week been like? Any of those pictures? Seeing family? Watching television? What's this one – going to the park?'

207

Pauline looked at the card, and looked at Amira. She looked at the other card, and held it up, pointing to the don't-want-to face.

'Don't want to!'

'Oh, yes, that's right, very good!'

'You don't want to tell us? That's fine, Pauline, that's fine. Okay. Can you pass the cards on to Mary there?'

'Mary?'

|

Mary's wheelchair had small wheels, like a shopping trolley. Anna had always pictured wheelchairs as having one large pair of wheels, so the user could propel themselves. She had seen people doing this. They wore special fingerless gloves. But perhaps this was only for younger wheelchair users. It would take some strength, pushing yourself around like that. If somebody else always did the pushing, perhaps it wasn't quite right to say Mary *used* a wheelchair. She was *sitting* in the wheelchair, sorting through the laminated cards.

'Right you are,' she said. 'Mary. Yes. Mary. Happy. Here.' Her voice was brisk, but slightly slurred. She held up the two cards in quick succession, pointing to the happy face and the picture of somebody watching television.

'Mary, hello. Welcome back to the group. So, you're happy today, and this week you've been watching television?'

'Yes. Yes.'

'Anything in particular you like to watch on the television, Mary?'

'They thunder all around, see, and bounder hup the final furlong there, you see.'

There was a pause in the room. Robert turned to look at Anna, with that crumpled look on his face that she had learned to recognise as concentration. Amira was nodding.

'Furlong,' she repeated. 'Is the word *furlong* from horse racing? Do you like to watch horse racing, Mary?'

'Yes, horse racing, yes. Thunder all around, and bounder hup.'

'Okay, great. Thank you, Mary.'

They worked their way around the circle. Wiktor showed everyone his name badge, and managed to explain that his name was spelled with a W but pronounced with a V. Robert said his name to the group, pointed vaguely at one of the faces, and passed the laminated cards straight on to Anna without saying anything more.

|

Liz kept an eye on the clock. The introductions were going well, but she could see people's attention drifting. Amira would need to bring them back. Robert's wife was passing the cards along to Sean, who looked as jumpy as ever. Her sessions with Sean had never made much progress, but his sheer energy had meant she'd always looked forward to them. He was committed, and convinced that his language was improving. He took the cards from Robert's wife, but Amira interrupted.

'Oh, I think we can all take part in the introductions,' she said, 'can't we?' Anna looked startled. Liz remembered the expression from their sessions, whenever she had suggested that all three of them could work on language strategies together.

'Sorry, Anna; is that okay? I'd like us all to take part, I think?'

'Yes, okay. Hello. I'm Anna Wright.' She looked at the laminated cards with a horrified expression. 'Sorry, I don't know.'

'How are you feeling today, Anna? Just, roughly?' There was a problem here. Liz could feel a tension rising in the room. People weren't distracted any more. Anna was struggling. Amira tried to prompt her. 'Just, *okay*, would you say?' Anna looked up, her eyes widening. Robert sighed loudly, and folded his arms.

'Sorry. Simple, really, isn't it? Okay. Okay.' She held the cards up, gesturing quickly at the emoji faces, and passed them along to Sean. As he grabbed them, and the attention of the room passed along, Liz watched Anna sink back into her chair, the colour rushing into her face as she stared down at the floor.

'Sean, welcome to the group. You're happy, that's good. Can you tell us something you've enjoyed doing this week?'

He looked back at Amira, still pointing at the happy emoji face. He was younger than his white hair made him look – forty-five or forty-six – with a lean and ropey look about him. Liz had never got to the bottom of what he'd done for a living before his stroke. She suspected that not all of it had been above board. There were photographs of his children in his wallet, which he'd told her were ten years out of date. There were pockmarks on his face. His lips moved silently while he processed what she had said.

'I do. I can. I, fucking, okay, sorry, fuck it.'

He turned the card over and around, making a gesture towards it that said: it's not here; the thing I want to tell you is not here.

'Can you describe it for us, Sean?'

'I can, I can, I do, I, what's this now, I fucking, sorry, like this now?' His swearing was compulsive and unintentional, and he flinched or shook his head each time. She'd told him he didn't need to keep apologising, but he couldn't shake the habit. He swung his arms like a runner, still sitting in his chair, puffing out his cheeks.

'Run! Running!' Pauline shouted.

'Yes yes,' Sean said, pointing to Pauline to say: that's it. She's got it. That's the one. 'Running. In the; out there.'

'You run outside. Do you have a particular place you like to go running, Sean?'

'No, I, I fucking run, see. Sorry. Every. All there.'

'You run everywhere?'

'Yes. Yes.'

'Okay, great. We'll have to add a running picture to the card. Thank you, Sean.'

He nodded, smiling, and passed the cards around the table. There was a clatter, and Robert stood up, as suddenly as he could manage. He walked unsteadily towards the door.

'You okay there, Robert?' Amira asked, quietly.

'Yes, yes, obviously, of course. Of course,' he said, without looking at her. Behind him, Anna had started to gather her coat and bag into her lap. Pauline called out goodbye, in a voice that Liz suspected was meant to be sarcastic, and Raymond said very good, very good. When Robert got to the door, Anna put her bag down again, and sat back in her chair. She made a small gesture, turning her hand over towards Amira, as if to say: actually, no, I'll stay here. Go ahead.

Amira smiled, and then covered the smile with her hand. Robert looked back into the room as the door closed behind him, with a storm of confusion across his face. Anna nodded.

'Okay. Thank you, Sean. And next to you we have Peter? Yes? Hello, Peter.'

Peter nodded, leaning forward and turning to look at everyone in the circle before he spoke. He straightened his tie, and nodded again.

'Yes. Yes we were, we came with you, all over, we were all over and the water was in you and with you, and the water he said to you, from there, the water you said and from here to there, you rode upon it over time and you were all under the water from here to here we are all once again and so it is, it is.'

'And how have you been feeling this week, Peter? Can you point to one of the faces on the card?'

He looked at Amira blankly, as though she hadn't yet spoken. Liz watched Robert walk up and down the corridor, glancing in at the door as he passed. Amira smiled, and tried again.

'Or could you tell us about something you've enjoyed doing this week, Peter? Something you like to do?'

'Something you like to do? Something you like to do. To do. Certainly we were all dreaming of the water from here to there and the you to him to her that came upon the water wished and well we wish you well and so the song she sing she sand she said again and then again it was what you said to me to she and then again you see, you see?'

'Thank you, Peter. Okay. Thank you.'

'Thanking you and now to you and thanking you and I do hope I hope the world is all for you and in the water where you go and the water there is all for you today.'

'Thank you, Peter. I hope so too. That's very kind of you to say.'

'And thanking you and you and you.'

3 |

Anna sat down in her usual chair, near the windows. She had a usual chair now. Everyone did. This was the fifth weekly meeting, and although they all knew each other's names they were still wearing the badges. She pinned hers to her cardigan, glancing down at the enthusiastic curves of Amira's handwriting. Robert's badge was on the table, in front of his empty chair. He would be here soon.

At the door, Peter was giving out the name badges, greeting everyone with his cheerful tumble of words. This was called fluent aphasia, it turned out. *Fluent* didn't seem the right word, when there was so little meaning. It came from *flow*, perhaps. Amira had started giving people responsibilities like this: Peter at the door, Wiktor making the coffee, Pauline arriving early to set out the chairs. Pauline was very precise about where she put the chairs. There was no job for Robert, yet.

'Hello to you and you and watch the water as it comes upon us all and here we are and another box becomes us unto where it is and so.'

'Sean, now. Tick the Sean box would you now, okay fucking come on, sorry, okay.'

'Hello to you and you.'

'Fucking hell, okay. Hello, so. Sorry.'

When they'd got off the bus Robert had sat down on a bench. He'd made a face to say he was a little winded, and gestured at her to go on ahead. The suggestion had felt absurd. She'd remembered Sara, at the age of six, announcing over breakfast that she would be going to school by herself from then on. I promise I definitely know the way, she'd said. You can get to work more earlier. But her husband was not a child. He'd looked at her, nodding. Obviously, obviously. Willing her to turn and walk away. She had done so. She hadn't looked back. She had left him on the bench, knowing he would struggle to ask for help or directions if he got stuck. Knowing that, really, he would be fine. Not turning around.

He had been doing things like this lately. Trying to prove himself. Trying to prove his independence. He no longer allowed her to help him get ready for bed, or get dressed in the morning. He put his own toast in the toaster. And last week when Bridget called round he had surprised them both by staggering into the room with a tray of tea and biscuits. He'd very nearly dropped it and she'd had to take it from him, but he'd then stood there nodding at them both until Bridget had asked, Jesus, Robert, is it a certificate you want or something?

It was still difficult to know what Robert made of these meetings. He had stopped leaving early, at least. Sara had asked him about it, the last time she was home, and Robert had sounded impatient. Not do much, he told her. Lots of *hello hello*. What, for? Games. Silly games. Hard, now, hear, what people say? Sara had laughed at him then, and said something about the pot calling the kettle black, and there had been a long pause before he'd laughed along with her.

Later she'd asked Anna why he wasn't talking properly yet. I thought he'd be getting better by now. I thought I'd see some improvement. This was deep into the evening, once Robert was settled in bed. Anna was loading the dishwasher, and cleaning the hob, and Sara was at the kitchen table with her phone, finishing a bottle of wine. Better how? Anna asked. Better in his language, his speech; I thought he'd be recovered by now, Sara said. It wasn't like a broken leg, Anna had to explain, again. It wasn't going to just heal. Hadn't she read the links Anna had sent? But I thought this group, Sara said; the practice. Therapy. Anna looked at her. Asked if she'd finished with the glass. Reminded her which was the recycling bin, and went up to bed.

Sara had a new job, and had split up with the boyfriend called Ace. Anna found it difficult to believe that was his real name. Frank had been promoted, although he'd told her the company had a flat hierarchy and they didn't call it promotion any more. There was a pay rise and he was working longer hours, Anna noted. *Promotion* seemed like exactly the right word. The two of them were both very busy.

Robert should be here by now. She looked out at the street. The sky was clouding over and the traffic was at a standstill. The park was empty, and the trees were bare. He would be stuck, if he tried to ask for help. She tried not to think of how impatient he would get, if he couldn't make himself understood.

His colleagues at the Institute had all set off for the summer season at Bluff Point, and it had been bothering him. Bridget had no time for this. He thinks he should be going down there with

them, is that it? Has he not had enough of all that now? He had
been down to the headquarters before everyone set off. Anna had
gone with him, and waited in reception while Brian took him on
a tour. He wasn't gone for long. As they were leaving, a group of
young people started loading kitbags into a minibus parked
outside. None of them spoke to Robert. They didn't recognise
him. Luke wasn't there.

Luke had come to the house again at the end of the summer,
before going to the training conference. He had some questions
about the new GPS equipment that he thought Robert would be
able to help him with. But when it seemed he was finished he said
there was actually one more thing. About the inquest, he said. I
wanted to apologise. For the way my parents were, you know?
They were just. They were upset. It was difficult for them. Anna
was confused by this. She didn't know what Luke was saying. It
was obvious that he had lied at the inquest, and lied to protect
Robert. She didn't know what he was apologising for now. There
was something else going on that she didn't understand. She'd
watched the two of them looking at each other.

The rain came, and the cars started flicking on their headlights, shining against the silvery tarmac. People started running,
holding bags and newspapers over their heads. She heard Robert
in the room behind her, telling Peter his name. When she turned
he was holding a takeaway coffee cup in one hand. He nodded in
her direction, and made his way across the room.

|

'Hello. Robert. This, me, here. Don't-want-to. Obviously, obviously. And, what. This week. Here. Computer. Robert, computer.'

'You've been working on the computer this week, Robert?'

'Yes, yes, well, obviously of course. Work.'

'And you're still the don't-want-to face?'

'Yes, yes. Obviously.'

'You don't want to be here, or you don't want to take part in these introductions?'

Robert looked at Amira and folded his arms. He had developed a very expressive way of doing this, she'd noticed.

'Robert?'

'Here. Don't-want-to. Here.'

'You don't want to be here?'

'Obviously, of course.'

'Okay. I hear that, Robert. But you are. You're here. You've been coming every week.'

'Yes, yes.'

'So. I'm just a little bit wondering why you're still coming if you don't want to be here?'

Robert made a puffing sound, blowing out his cheeks and throwing his hands up in the air: I can't explain it, Amira thought he was saying. You're asking too much. You're asking the impossible.

'I mean, we're glad to have you. But I'm just curious.'

'Wife,' he blurted out, throwing a glance towards Anna.

'Sorry?'

'Wife, coming, here. Obviously. Christ, obviously, me come here now, and, also. She *tell* me. Obviously. *Tell* me. Pull me. Of course. Only, only.'

'You only come here because Anna makes you?'

'Yes! Christ. Obviously. Of course.'

'I'm not sure that's fair, Robert. I imagine she thinks you might get something out of coming here? She thinks you both might get something out of it?'

'Yes! Only. Only biscuits!'

Some people laughed at this, and the laughter allowed the moment to pass. There seemed to be a misconception that he had made a joke. But Amira watched his expression and saw no humour in it.

After the introductions, she explained that she wanted to explore ways of talking about things they had done in their lives. Before their strokes, and now.

'Mary, I've been told you've always had an interest in horses, is that right?' She held up a series of postcards, with pictures of different horses: a horse grazing in a field, a shire horse pulling a cart, a showjumping horse in the ring. Mary was looking at the pictures with a narrow expression. She shook her head dismissively.

'Horses, Mary!'

'Oh yes, that's right.'

'Did you used to ride horses, Mary?' Amira asked, passing the pictures around the table.

'My span I wanted the wash inside,' said Mary, firmly.

'Did you ride a horse? Like this?'

'Wash inside the wheel while we work, we walk and so on.'

'But you did something with horses, you worked with them?'

Mary nodded, pointing at Amira, and then pointing around the room in a large, slow circle. There, she meant: all around, a circle, all around.

'In case the sluggish tithes come out tonight,' she said.

'Can anyone help us here? Is there one of these pictures that might help us? Pauline, what do you have there?'

'Jumping! Mary! This, this, showjumping, is it?'

Mary looked at the picture Pauline was showing her, and shook her head again. Pauline started to say something else, but Mary lifted a finger to stop her, turning her head to see if anyone else had a suggestion. Amira sometimes wondered if Mary thought these were board meetings of some sort.

'Mary, could you show us something? Something you used to do with horses?'

|

Amira had got up from her seat, and was crouching in the stance of a jockey. She asked Mary if she had ridden horses, like this, and Mary looked back at her with a stern expression. Liz could see that she was uncomfortable with the play-acting. She'd got the impression, from a brief conversation with Mary's daughter, that Mary hadn't been a particularly playful person, before her stroke. When Amira had talked about using mime and move-ment in today's session, Liz had wondered if they might want to hold back.

'What other actions do people do, when they're working with horses? Anyone?'

'Yes, okay, like this, see. Shit, shit, like this, see?' Sean was making a two-handed digging gesture. Raymond pointed at him in agreement.

'Right, like mucking out the stables do you mean, Sean?'

'Yes, okay, mucking. Mucking. Like this, see? Mary?'

'Oh yes, that's right! Very good.'

Mary gave Raymond and Sean both a look, and shook her head.

'My simple certain then became,' she said, sharply.

'You didn't work in the stables then,' Amira said. 'Could you tell us what you did do? Are any of these pictures helpful?'

Mary sorted through the pictures in front of her. Sean and Raymond were still talking about mucking out stables. Mary found a picture of a man in a suit leading a racehorse away from a row of stables. There was a jockey on the horse, leaning forward to pat the horse's neck.

'The shiver shook the brook,' Mary explained.

'So you worked with racehorses, in particular?'

Mary shook her head. 'With money later, later circle by the final furlong, hup.'

'Were you a trainer?'

Mary nodded slowly, with a distant look in her eyes. Liz noticed how excited Sean was by this news; he started asking Mary for the names of horses she'd trained, and whether she'd ever won big. Mary sat back in her chair and looked around the room. She was happy to have the attention.

'Refinery,' she said. 'Refinery is the boiler to sieve again and again, do you see?'

'No wonder you enjoy watching horse racing on the television now.'

'Oh yes!' agreed Raymond. 'Yes, that's right. Very good, very good!'

221

'Again, again, the coming noise upon,' said Peter. 'And then we were and all upon us so we were, we were.'

|

There was a general outbreak of conversation. Amira imagined writing this in her notes, and smiled. *General outbreak of conversation.* Pauline was up and rearranging her chair, and her sister was asking her not to, please. Wiktor was working his way across the room to the coffee machine. Robert had turned to Raymond and was saying something about a red plane. Raymond was agreeing, but Barbara leaned across him and asked Robert to explain. Sean was trying to talk to Mary about the racehorses. Amira watched them all. *A general outbreak of conversation.* She went back to her chair, and waited for the group to settle.

'So. Now. Thank you, Mary. It was good to hear some of your story. And I can see that some of you have stories of your own to tell. We all like telling stories, don't we? What have you done today? What did you see on your way to the shops? Where did you go on your holidays? We tell stories all the time, don't we?'

'Oh yes! Very good. Very good.'

'Don't want to! Don't, don't. No words words!'

'Of course, Pauline. Absolutely. Telling stories is part of what's difficult about living with aphasia. Of course it is.'

'Tricksy fucking words, sorry, like fucking broken see, sorry sorry.'

'It's okay, Sean. You're right to be frustrated. But we're starting to think about different ways of communicating, aren't we? And you're each working to find your own techniques. We don't always have the words. But we can talk around things. We can use gestures. We've done some singing. We can think about drawing, and writing. We could even think about movement; about dance?'

'No, fucking, sorry; what now?'

'Don't laugh, Sean; we'll have you dancing, I'm sure.'

'Yeah you will you will you so. Come on now.'

'Dancer! Sean! Dancer! For money?'

Sean turned to Pauline, tilting his head and leaning into a song about being a private dancer. His voice was unexpectedly smooth and clear, and the words came easily. As he sang the first line his eyes lit up in surprise.

'Oh yes! Very good, Sean, very good! That's right.'

He would do what they wanted him to do, he sang, and then stopped abruptly, as though he'd only just noticed what he was doing.

'Fucking, sorry, what are you all about now,' he said, his voice trailing away as the room broke into laughter and applause.

4 |

Liz had wondered, all through the planning of this, whether it might be seen as a cruelty to bring dancers into the room at all. The bare facts of their youth and health could be taken as an affront. They weren't *dancers*, in this context; they were movement therapists, and she understood the skills and experience they would bring to the sessions. She had helped to write the funding applications. But still, as they came into the room, practically flowing through the door, they made even Amira look stiff and awkward by comparison. Their movements were sprung and light, and their body language was a kind of purr. Only one of them accepted the offer of coffee. The other two had brought their own herbal teabags. Their voices were soft, and their bodies were hard, and Liz imagined that some in the room would soon be besotted.

There had been a lot of discussion about risk, during the planning stages. The mention of *dance* in the context of people with limited mobility – people who used sticks and walking frames, or whose bodies could fail in sudden and unpredictable ways – had caused some concern. But Amira had insisted that using total communication to explore storytelling needed to involve as much movement as possible. More movement than people might have become used to, she'd said. I'd like to stretch people's ideas of what's possible. Which was fine, but they'd still had to write out a risk assessment for each member of the group, and set down what movements would or wouldn't be viable.

|

People were taking longer to settle this morning, understandably. Amira had set the chairs out without the tables, and made sure that the dancers were interspersed among the group. People were saying nothing to the dancers, and glancing at them constantly.

Amira reminded everyone that they'd talked about doing some movement work today, and asked them all to keep an open mind. She introduced the dancers – Gavin, Rachel, and Charmaine – and passed around the laminated cards. Raymond went first. He was on his own today, and his voice was quieter than usual.

'Raymond. Hello. Yes. Happy. Very good, very good. And. And this one here, that's right, very good.'

He pointed to the happy face, and to a picture of a sandcastle on a beach and children running into the sea.

'You've been to the beach, Raymond?'

'Oh, yes. That's right. Very good. Very good. Beach. Yes.'

'In this weather?'

'Ha! Ha! No, no. Like that, you see, like—' He swept one hand up past his body and away into the air in a high curve, meaning something like: away, gone, flying.

225

'You went abroad? On holiday? Where did you go?'

'That's right, yes, very good. Very good.'

'Where did you go, Raymond?'

'Ah, now. Ja, ja, ja.' He jerked his head on each syllable, trying to shake the word out. Amira tried to help.

'Jamaica? You've been back to Jamaica? Oh, I bet that was lovely.'

'Ha! Ha! No, no, no. Like that, you see. Ja, ja.'

He jabbed towards the floor, still searching for the word.

'Down? Somewhere south? Ja, ja. Anyone?' Amira glanced at the rest of the group, inviting them to help.

'Japan!'

'Jaipur!'

'Ja, ja, yes, very good. Like that, you know.'

'Jersey?' Raymond turned and pointed to Carol when she said this. He looked delighted.

'Yes! That's true. Very good. Jersey. That's right.'

'You went to Jersey? Well, it won't have been swimming weather there, will it? At this time of year?'

|

Anna tried to imagine taking Robert on holiday. The thought of it was exhausting. She understood why Barbara had brought Raymond to the door and then left him. The woman would need a holiday of her own. She looked at Robert, who was leaning forward and waiting for his turn to speak. He wanted to take part in the group now. He had pinned his name badge to his jacket, and said hello to people. These were all things to be pleased about, Bridget had told Anna. Focus on what's going well. She was right, probably. It had been a difficult week. Robert had been preoccupied by the teams travelling down to Bluff Point, and especially by who might be working at Station K. He had found a selection of webcams on the Institute website. The images were grainy and uneventful, but they held him enthralled. *Enthralled* was the wrong word. He couldn't look away but he hated it. He was angry. There was more crying. He had been sent a copy of the Institute's incident report on Thomas's death, and was slowly reading it over and over again. Sometimes when he read it he would jab at particular words on the page. *Radio*, or *protocol*, or *adverse*. Frank had seen a copy, and was keen to explain to her that it contained no findings of responsibility. She told him she knew how to read a report. Okay, sorry, but Mum; whatever happened down there was not his fault – does he understand that? Anna had pointed out that the report only showed a lack of evidence of anyone being to blame. Mum, bloody hell, what are you trying to say?

She wasn't *trying* to say anything.

Frank had been home for the weekend, and while he was there she'd asked him to stay with Robert so she could go to meeting. It was her first time back for months. Nobody asked her about Robert, as she'd feared. They said hello, and left her alone. The silence of the meeting was such a relief. A silence with no expectations. She sat, and everyone sat, and there were all these shifts and settlings in the room. Something happened, and nothing happened, and she decided she would go back more often.

Robert was listening to the introductions. He was holding the laminated card and telling the rest of the group that he was fine,

227

that he had been working on a computer this week. He passed her the cards, and she said what she was expected to say.

|

There was just what they called hand work, to start with. Three of them paired with a dancer, while the rest of the group watched. Each pair sat facing each other with their hands almost touching. Amira said they were to mirror each other's movements, and to keep at least the tips of their fingers touching. She demonstrated briefly with one of the dancers. Their hands moved up, and down, and out to the side: fingers spread, fingers together, fingers clenched into a fist, one single finger touching, barely touching. The movements were slow but smooth, and it was difficult to see who was leading.

Liz stood and moved a little closer. There was music, quietly, and they began.

Mary was talking a lot. Her hand didn't always do what she wanted it to. It carried a trembling motion that her partner, Gavin, gently mirrored. It was difficult to keep their fingertips in contact. Between them they raised the awkward couple of their hands, up above their heads and then slowly down to their knees. Gavin watched her. The eye contact was part of the routine. When Mary tried to look away, Gavin went with her and held her gaze. His smile was gentle and constant. For a moment it was easy to forget that the exercise was about hands at all, watching the way Gavin had to dip and weave to keep himself in Mary's eyeline. I'm here, he was saying, silently. Stay with me, Mary. I've got you.

'Were the skirtly saucer down?' Mary asked. 'Were the skirtly saucer down? And there it were.'

Gavin smiled, and held her gaze. Mary's right hand was limp in her lap, as always, but her left hand was alive in the air.

'Went the weft the way we were,' she said.

Her movements were still slow and jerky, but Gavin was taking this staccato rhythm and absorbing it into something slowly fluid. As their movements developed a pattern, Mary relaxed into the hold of his eye contact.

'Winter wear we waited for,' she murmured.

The music in the room was faint, barely rising above the snatches of talk and the traffic outside. Liz watched the concentration on Robert's face. He was copying his partner, Charmaine, even to the point of dipping his shoulder each time their hands changed direction. He wanted to get this right.

'Intact we were and all becoming,' Mary said, confidently.

After a few minutes they stopped, and the dancers changed partners. Liz had suggested putting Peter in this second group, so that he could watch the first group and understand what to do, but he still struggled. His care worker sat with him and tried to explain, and he nodded without understanding at all. He sat opposite Rachel, and when she held her right hand up with the palm towards him, he held up his own right hand. She tried to swap hands, and he did the same, and when she patiently tried to touch her hand to his, he moved his hand across to the other side.

Pauline was distracted by Peter's misunderstanding, and kept leaning over to get his attention.

'Pete! Petey! Peter, no! No, no! This hand, Pete, this hand, see,

see, see? This hand? He's wrong, he's wrong. He's doing. Pete! Pete!'

Amira went over and reassured her, but she couldn't settle. She stood up and moved her chair around, and Gavin moved his, but she still kept twisting around to see what Peter was doing.

Each time Rachel tried to reach Peter's hand he simply copied her movements from the other side. Rachel went with it, and began extending the range of her movements.

'Well here we are and one and all with our hands in the water and down we go, do you see, do you see, down and away we go to the sea and then they look around and down and upside down inside the water while around the bubbles up and bubbles down the water in the water while we wave you see, you see, do you see?'

They lifted their hands above their heads, down to the floor, out to the side. As Rachel stretched out to her left, she appeared to move into a blind spot on Peter's right. His hand simply paused at the edge of this blind spot, as if that space didn't exist for him, and waited for her hand to return. And all the time he was smiling, contented, keeping up his side of the conversation.

'So I hope the world will be all around the waves for you and you and you and here it is to be where we will come again into the world the waves the water where we were to be, you see, you know?'

Around the room the resistance and the agitation was ebbing away, and as it did so the dancers began softly to synchronise their movements, each pair shadowing the one beside them and the one beside that. The movements found an awkward, hesitant kind of flow. There was an air of surprise in the room. When the music stopped, there was a reluctance at first to lower their hands and break contact.

'Fucking yeah okay that'll fucking do,' Sean said.

5 |

Pauline didn't come back, after that first week with the dancers. Amira went to see her but she wouldn't be persuaded. She was angry and frustrated and the conversation was short. Her sister was there, and came out to the car, and Amira asked her to let Pauline know she was always welcome. She just wants proper speech therapy though, Carol said. She wants to get on with it; none of this other business.

Amira had expected setbacks but this was difficult. She had thought the group was making progress, and that Pauline was a part of that. Liz said she shouldn't take it personally, but it was difficult to shake off the casual way Carol had dismissed her. Something about that word *proper*. She wants proper speech therapy. Like Amira hadn't thought it all through. Like I'm just playing at this, she told Liz. It was a bit like: let me speak to the manager. You know what I mean?

Liz didn't know what she meant, apparently.

But everyone else had stuck with it, and got used to the dancers being there. It helped when they realised no one was going to make them do anything they might think of as *dancing*. She should have avoided the word altogether.

It was possible they had even started to enjoy it. They were quicker to take their seats at the start of each session, and rattled through the checking in. Happy, yes, shopping, yes, that's right, next.

Rachel generally took the lead. She had them doing warm-ups in their chairs: wriggling fingers, shaking arms, stretching towards the ceiling, waggling their whole bodies from side to side. She was cautious about asking people to stand. When she had suggestions about movements, she didn't just tell them but worked around the room and showed them what she meant. Straightening arms, stretching out fingertips, turning shoulders from side to side. She had a way of negotiating permission through her touch; ready to withdraw if she felt reluctance, but confident and firm enough that any reluctance was stilled. This kind of touch was unusual for some people here, Amira suspected. They were more used to being steered and guided. *Safely handled.*

Gavin worked closely with Mary, helping her learn how much she could manage from her chair, and Charmaine stayed close to Peter. He had a lot to say but spoken instructions were often no help. He needed to feel his body doing a movement before he was able to repeat it. Once he understood an action his movements were sometimes the most fluid in the group.

Today, Amira wanted them to think about using movement to communicate story. Their stories. She needed to be careful about how this was phrased, and how it would be heard. But she thought they would be ready. She turned on the coffee machine, and set out the name badges on the table by the door.

|

Robert's movement was improving. He still used the stick, but he was back to being able to stride ahead of Anna in the way she had always been used to. She had found it infuriating for years, but it was almost comforting to see him doing it again. She followed him along the corridor. By the time she caught up with him, he was already taking his name badge from Peter, and making his way to his usual seat. Wiktor was seeing to the coffees. Amira came over to meet her, and said that actually today they were going to try something a little bit different. They wanted to ask all the supporters to take a break, and come back at the end of the session. Would that be okay with her? It would maybe create something of a different atmosphere, a different energy?

Anna looked at Robert. He was saying something to Raymond, and Raymond was agreeing enthusiastically. One of the dancers was passing him a coffee. He hadn't noticed that she wasn't with him. She saw him tap Raymond's arm and say something, the two of them breaking into laughter, and she told Amira that yes, of course, that would be fine. She tried to say goodbye to Robert, but she couldn't catch his eye.

Luke had been in touch again, asking about doing a video call from Station K. They had installed a new satellite link, and he wanted to show Robert. Anna didn't think Robert would like the idea. But Sara was up at the weekend, and she helped to arrange it. There was nothing complicated to arrange, in the end. She clicked on an email and then Luke was there, on the screen, in the room, standing outside the red field hut at Station K. The mountains and the ridges and the blue sky behind him. It made Anna and Sara very quiet for a moment. They had seen so many of Robert's photos, but this made it seem much closer, and suddenly more real. Before Robert could start talking, she leaned over him and asked Luke to show them around. He held up his phone and turned in a long, slow circle. They saw the hut, the stores, the toilet block, the long scree flank of Garrard Ridge, the snow vapour blowing off the top of the Everard Glacier in the distance. She recognised all of it from his maps and photographs and hours of conversation. Luke started telling Robert about the satellite installation. He told Robert they spent their evenings watching cat videos on Facebook now, and it was clear from Sara's response that he was making a joke. Teasing Robert. Robert nodded, and said *ha*, and asked about the condition of the skiway. There were glitches and pauses in the connection. When they'd finished, Robert didn't say anything. Sara had made a note of Luke's email address, in case anything needed following up.

As she came out of the building she saw the trees moving in the wind, the last of their leaves breaking loose and flapping wetly to the ground. The traffic bunched and shifted, windows steamed against the drizzle. She opened her umbrella, and cut across the road towards the park. She wasn't sure where to go. She'd forgotten what to do with free time.

She could find a coffee shop, and catch up on emails. Work had been feeling less urgent since she'd been left off the lists of named investigators on the new funding bids, but there were still emails to catch up on. Her research director had said her work would always be valued. As soon as your situation changes and you're able to commit the time, there'll be a primary role available for you, she said. This is no reflection. It would just be unfair to burden you at this difficult time. They had given her a year's teaching leave. Her focus now was on public engagement. She had spent some time dealing with Freedom of Information requests.

She could stay close in case she was needed, in case Amira called and said something had gone wrong. She could phone Sara and Frank while she was waiting, and make sure they were okay. There was a whole series of people she should call. Or she could do none of those things.

She glanced up behind her at the row of tall windows on the second floor, and walked through the park. She turned right when she got to the riverbank, and walked out along the path, away from the town, out of reach.

|

'Sean, I'm going to ask you to just fall backwards, and I'll catch you, okay?'

'What's that now, fucking, what's. Sorry. Who now?'

'Let yourself fall, okay? Lean back. Lean, lean, lean. Fall. There. See? I've got you.'

'Oh Jesus now. Fucking. Sorry. Fucks. Sorry. Robert, hey. Robert. You, you. Big man. You. Come on now, fucking. Sorry.'

'Oh, yes, very good! That's right, very good.'

'Sean? Sean, let's try again. Robert can go next. Okay. Keep your back straight. Don't look behind you. Lean, lean. Fall. That's it. Once more.'

'Would you not now. So, okay. Okay.'

'That's it. Lean; fall. Okay?'

|

They talked about stories again. Amira had tried to keep the idea of stories running through these meetings, talking about how they all had their own stories, and people would like to hear those stories, and might it be interesting to think of different ways they could get their stories out into the world?

'Robert?'

His attention had drifted, Liz could see: to the window, to the movement of the trees, to the traffic on the road below. He turned when he heard his name, and sat a little straighter in his chair.

'Yes, yes.'

'Robert, can you tell us something about yourself? Can you tell us what you were doing before you had your stroke?'

'Yes, well obviously. Yes.'

'I think we've all picked up bits and pieces over the course of these meetings, but could you tell us a bit more? What was your job?'

Robert nodded while he processed the question, closing his eyes in concentration.

'Robert,' he said. He held one hand across his chest: here I am, I'm talking about me, Robert. 'Robert. Wok. Guy, guy.' He unfolded an imaginary map in his lap, tracing a line across it, pointing into the far distance before hoisting a pack onto his back. 'Ex, ex, expo. Expo.' He tapped his chest to dislodge the word. 'Guide.'

'That's right! Very good, very good.'

Liz was disappointed that Anna wasn't there to see this. After all his reluctance, she thought Anna would appreciate seeing Robert now, the centre of attention, telling his story.

'You work as a guide, Robert? Let's all just listen to Robert for a moment.'

'Yes. Support. Assist. Hmm. Ant. Assistant.' He waved his fist in frustration. 'Tech, tech. Support. For export. No. Guide, for. For expanded. No, no. Christ.'

'I think I know the word you mean, Robert. A guide for ex—?'

'Caress again the waves and water carving through the veins?'

'It's, no, not quite. I don't think that's quite what Robert's looking for, Peter, but thank you.'

'And thanking you and you and all to you.'

'Expeditions?'

'Yes, yes, obviously well obviously of course. Expert. Expo. Guide.'

'Expeditions, okay, great, thank you Rachel. So, you're an expedition guide. You do technical support for expeditions? In this country?'

Amira knew full well where Robert had worked. Liz had talked it through with her, including the inquest and the sensitivity around those events.

Robert shook his head and pointed to the floor. Pointing south.

'Ant, ant, ant.' He puffed out his cheeks in desperation. He rubbed his arms and shivered in mock cold.

'Antarctica?' Amira said, softly. Robert nodded, and pointed to her, pointing to the word she had just said as though it were still hanging in the air in front of them all.

'Ant, ark.'

'You were a guide in Antarctica?'

'Yes, yes, yes.'

'Well, that's something new. Has anyone else been to Antarctica?'

'Oh, that's right! Very good!'

'Does anyone have questions for Robert, about working there? About living there, I suppose. Did you stay there for a long time, Robert?'

'Yes, yes, obviously. Yes. One, two, three, four. Moon, moon. Christ! Moons.'

'Months? Four months?'

'Yes, yes of course. Of course.'

'Four months at a time? Was this once, or lots of times?'

'Yes, yes. More. More.' He marked out a series of intervals by chopping at the air with his hand.

'Lots of times? Every year?'

'Yes, yes. Obviously.'

'Oh, very good!'

'So, who has questions for Robert, about Antarctica? Sean?'

'Is it, is it fucking cold now, sorry, cold now?'

'Christ! Yes. Yes. Code.'

Rachel stood in front of Robert, and asked him to stand. She asked him to show her how it felt to be cold, to be outside in Antarctica. Robert nodded. He mimed putting on a coat, and gloves, and balaclava.

'Wear this. Warm. Coats. Head, coat. Hand, coats. Christ! No. Hmm, hmm. Hand, hand.'

'Gloves?'

'Yes, yes!'

'So you're wearing protective clothing, lots of clothing.'

'Yes, obviously. Of course.'

Rachel echoed his mime of putting on the clothes, and as she did so her body expanded with the extra layers.

'And does it feel cold when you go outside?'

Robert puffed out his cheeks and blew, leaning forwards into an imaginary strong wind.

'Code. Code. This. Here. This.' He blew hard, and staggered. Rachel staggered beside him, her movements encumbered.

'It's windy?'

'Yes!'

'Very windy. And that makes it feel colder? Okay. And so what do you do to stay warm?'

'Ha! Here, here, here. Yes. Yes. Here.' He staggered across the room, swinging his arms.

'You?'

'Yes! Yes. On, on. Christ.'

'Oh, you keep moving?'

'Yes!'

'You have to keep moving to stay warm?'

'Yes, obviously, yes, of course.'

'Okay. And you get back into the – what? The base, the hut? As quick as you can?'

'Yes, yes.'

'Robert! Is there fucking, sorry, what you say fucking how you know little birds, little birds.'

'Oh, that's right! Very good!'

'Fucking, sorry, little birds, jackets, what.'

Sean was doing a waddling motion in his seat, screwing up his face while he searched for the word.

'Penguins, Sean?'

'Too right, fuck it, yes, sorry, peng, peng.'

'Penguins.'

'Penguins. Fucking yes. Sorry.'

'Did you see penguins, Robert?'

'Ah, yes. No. Ant, ant. Yes. Me, no.' He drew a circle in the air, pointing first to the top of it and then somewhere further down.

'They have penguins in Antarctica, don't they?'

'Christ! Yes. Yes! But me, no. No.'

'Not where you were working?'

'Yes, yes, of course.' He drew the circle again, and pointed to somewhere inside it.

'Oh, this is a map? This is Antarctica? And you worked somewhere, what, further south?'

'Oh, that's right!'

'And there are no penguins there?'

'No, no. Obviously. No.'

'Too cold for the fucking, sorry, is it now?'

'Robert, do you have maps at home, of Antarctica?'

'Obviously, yes.'

'Will you bring them in next week, and show us? And maybe bring some pictures as well? Tell us more about what it's like working there?'

Robert shrugged, and nodded. Amira thanked him, but he waved his hand in front of his face.

'No. No. But, but. Hard. Now. Words, now.' He puffed out his cheeks and blew.

'It's hard to talk about things, Robert. I know. It's hard to put them into words?'

'Oh yes, that's right!'

'Fucking is it is.'

Robert rubbed his face, slowly. He turned to go back to his seat, losing his balance as he did so. He leaned to one side, and just as it seemed he was falling, Rachel was beside him and holding his weight. She helped him back into his seat. Nobody spoke. The wind moved through the bare branches of the trees outside, and their shadows moved across the floor.

6 |

'No, we're going through the answers now, okay?'

'Number seven?'

'No, we're on number eight. Seven was Bletchley Park. The codebreaking centre. Everyone got that, Bletchley Park?'

'Oh yes, very good. That's right, very good.'

'Okay, number eight was: who was Shakespeare's wife?'

Amira had booked the room for longer this week, and started things off with a quiz. She'd asked the dancers to come later, after the break. She thought people could do with a change of pace. The movement sessions had been going well, but they were intense. She had thought people would resent the dance therapists' mobility, but in fact it had done something quite different. People were finding their own ways to move. There were no miracles, but it sometimes shook loose emotions. It was something close to what she'd been aiming for, but she had mixed feelings. It made her feel manipulative. Stirring things up for these people, maybe for nothing. She kept thinking about Pauline's sister saying she just wanted *proper speech therapy*.

The quiz was going well, though. Asking the questions had been noisy and chaotic, and she wasn't sure she'd pitched them right. But the main point of the exercise was to have had them working in pairs, and they were doing that.

'Shakespeare's wife: anyone?' She looked around the room. Sean was just trying to pronounce the name. Mary was smiling confidently, with Raymond gesturing at her to speak up.

'Anyone? Mary?'

'Annie and away we go to the wall to the wall,' she said, putting down her pen and folding her hands neatly together.

'Try again, Mary? I think you're there.' Mary looked at her, patiently, as though she was waiting for Amira to understand.

'No, no, no!' Sean said, suddenly. He had something to contribute.

'Sean? Sean and Wiktor, do you have something?'

'Muh, muh, muh, fucking, sorry.' The little shake of the head Sean did each time he swore was still there. Wiktor watched him.

'Sean has good answer, I think,' he said.

'Oh, that's right, very good,' said Raymond, encouragingly.

'Muh. Missus. Missus!'

'What's that?'

'Mrs Shaykuh spear!'

'Mrs Shakespeare, that's it, very good! Very good!'

|

Sara was home for the week, and had asked to go with Robert to the group. There had been some delay getting out of the house, and they'd missed the bus. Robert was fuming. The bus had been running early, but when Sara pointed this out he wasn't interested. It was still her fault. They would have to wait half an hour for the next one, in this weather. He had never been very good at waiting.

Anna watched the two of them sitting side by side in the bus shelter, their heads tucked down into their coats like moody teenagers. It reminded her of how much Sara had always resented taking the school bus; how she'd resented Anna for having moved them to that house in the middle of nowhere in the first place, resented them for not having a car, resented her dad for not being around at all. She had carried a lot of resentment around at that age. She'd mostly expressed it through silence, and slammed doors, and black hair dye.

Sara broke the silence first. She asked Robert how the group meetings were going, and what they were doing now. He sighed dramatically, looking at his watch and telling her they would be late.

'Okay, Dad, I've got that. But tell me about the group?'

He puffed out his cheeks and turned his hands over, in the way that he did when he meant: I don't know, it's hard to explain, what do you want me to say? She asked if he liked the other people there, and he shrugged.

'Okay,' he said. 'Okay.'

Frank had asked about it, the last time he'd called. What's he getting out of going to that group? he'd asked; have you noticed his speech getting any better? There was something suspicious about it, he seemed to be implying. Somebody was on the make. She wasn't sure what anyone could be making out of what happened in the group.

His speech is just about the same, she'd told Frank, and he'd said *exactly my point* in the same infuriating tone he'd always had when he thought he'd been proven right.

Sara had the same questions. She hadn't been home for a while. She'd been busy at work and said it was difficult to get away. But she'd also admitted that she found it hard to see Robert like this: hesitant and stumbling, repeating the same few phrases. The anger that flashed across his face when she didn't understand what he was trying to say. The way he kept turning impatiently away from people. Anna said she hadn't noticed him doing this, exactly, and Sara had said that no, she didn't imagine she had.

'I heard they've got you doing dancing, Dad, in the group?'

Robert shook his head briskly.

'No, no, no. Not dance. No. Moving. Moving.'

This was an important distinction for him, Anna knew.

'Moving, then. And how's that going?'

Another shrug, and then the bus arrived.

When they got to the centre she let Sara go in and take Robert upstairs. She watched them move through the corridor towards the lift, Robert leaning hard on his stick and trying to stride ahead. She turned away, and went for her usual walk along the river. Something Sara had said earlier was still bothering her. They'd been talking about Luke, and the inquest, and Sara said that when she'd asked Luke why he hadn't told the Institute more about what had happened, he'd just asked who she thought they would listen to, really. Anna asked what he might have meant by that. It seemed to allude to something but she didn't understand what. Isn't it obvious, Mum?

For as long as she could remember people had been telling her things were obvious. They rarely were.

|

'I'll give you a point for that, Sean. It's not actually the answer we're looking for, but well done. Everyone else, two points if you got Anne Hathaway. I think you got that, Mary?'

'And away we go to the wall to the wall.'

'Can you read what you've written down there, Mary?'

'Anne. Anne Hath. A. Way.'

'Exactly! Well done. Okay. And here's Robert, hello Robert, hi.'

The young woman with him was his daughter, presumably. Amira could see something of Anna in her, but with more confidence. More eye contact. She went to greet them both, and explained to Robert that they were just finishing off a quiz. You could take a seat with Peter there, she said, and introduced herself to the young woman.

'Hi, I'm Sara, I'm Robert's daughter. Should I; I'll come back for him around, what, twelve o'clock?' She was looking past Amira as she spoke, towards Robert, not trusting that he would be fine.

'Actually, why don't you stay?' She'd said this before she thought about it. There was something about Sara's manner. It would be good for her to see her father in this environment, Amira thought.

'Would that be okay? It's not, you know, private?'

'Supporters usually come back later, but I'm happy to make an exception.'

'Well, okay then. I'll just—'

'Take a seat over there by the windows, if you like, with Liz?'

'Okay. Right. No problem.' Sara walked over to the corner and unstacked one of the chairs. Amira saw her trying to catch

Robert's eye on her way past, and Robert instead looking intently at Peter while he tried to follow what Peter was saying. She moved to the centre of the circle and brought their attention back to the quiz.

'Oh, this would have been an easy one for you, Robert, if you'd been here. This was number nine. Number nine. Who was the first man to reach the South Pole?'

'Ha! Christ! Obviously, obviously.'

'Exactly, Robert, yes. I thought you'd know it. Peter, is that your hand up? Do you have an answer?'

'We went so we did under all the weight of where the world was over us and the long day the long wild day you see it came it came and the wind blew long and the night was gone for you for me and so it went and there it went upon the end of the earth for you for me, you see?'

'Well, thank you Peter. Does anyone have a different answer?'

'And thanking you and you and you, you see.'

'Scott! Great Scott!' Sean said, slamming his hand down on the table.

'No, I can see Robert shaking his head there. It certainly wasn't poor old Scott, was it? Have you got the answer?'

'Yes, of course. Am, am. Am.'

'Have you written it down already? Mary, can you read what Robert has written?'

'Ah – mund – sen is whipped and cold comes the curl.'

'Amundsen, excellent. He was Norwegian, wasn't he, Robert?'

'Yes, yes of course.'

'And rather better prepared than Scott, I understand.'

'Ha! Christ. Christ. Yes.'

'Did you ever go?'

'Hmm. So, so.'

'To the South Pole, I mean?'

'Ha! No. No. Long, far.'

He drew a circle in the air, pointing to the edge and to himself, and then pointing to the centre.

'It was too far from where you were working?'

'Ha! Christ, yes, yes, obviously, of course.'

'Is five, fucking, sorry. Is five hundred miles, is it?'

'Oh, that's right! Very good.'

'Yes, yes, well, obviously. More, more.'

Sean broke into song again, singing about how he would walk five hundred miles. When he knew a song well the words came clear and unbroken, and he took great pleasure in the fact. And he would walk five hundred more, he sang.

'Thank you, Sean. Lovely. Okay.'

|

'Can you tell us a little bit about your life before the stroke, Wiktor?'

Wiktor shrugged, his eyes turned to the floor. He was standing in the middle of the circle, facing Amira. He had taken some time to move forward but there had been no reluctance. He was ready for this now, Liz thought. He had planted his stick with force beside him. His arm trembled with the strain of standing up straight. It was a strong arm.

'Liz told me that you worked in IT, didn't you? Was that here, in Cambridge? What did you do?'

Another shrug, slightly different this time: I could tell you but it wouldn't be important. I could tell you but you wouldn't understand. It's difficult to put into words.

'Are you able to use computers now, Wiktor? Is that still a part of your life?'

He screwed up his face. A different shrug again: his head dipping slowly, his shoulders curled. A shrug that said: I can, or I cannot. It's complicated. It's hard to explain.

Wiktor often resorted to shrugging. Liz had noted this from their first sessions. She had tried to work with him on it. He seemed to think that his shrugs had more of an expressive range than they actually did. Could you find another way of responding, Wiktor?

Rachel quietly stepped alongside him and began to mirror these shrugs. For a moment Liz wondered if she was mocking him. But there was something more delicate about what she was doing. She was amplifying his movements; taking them on for herself. Lifting her shoulders, dropping her head. Pushing her lip out and down. Wiktor stopped. Liz watched him waver on the edge of affront.

'Ha,' he said, once.

Rachel circled around to face him, and now he lifted his face to meet her eyes. Amira kept asking questions, and then Rachel started to join in, the two of them taking turns in a pattern that almost became a song:

'What was your life like before your stroke, Wiktor?'
'What was your life like before?'
'Can you tell us more of your experiences?'
'Can you tell us more about how you feel?'

250

The other dancers stood beside Wiktor, facing the group, and leading the shrugs: lifting their shoulders, turning their palms towards the ceiling, dropping their heads. It started to take on a rhythm. The group leader was stamping her feet with each of the shrugs, carefully feeding the beat. Robert's daughter took out her phone and started filming, and Liz had to ask her to stop.

'What are your medium- and short-term goals?'

'What. You life before?'

'You want,' Robert said, 'you want, wok?' He was leaning towards Wiktor and Rachel, his voice loud and clear. 'Wok, wok, you want to work again?' Wiktor and the dancers all looked at him and shrugged once more, and Robert shrugged in return. He looked very pleased with himself.

Peter straightened his tie, and started speaking.

'Will you wade with me in the water now Wiktor, will you wade in to your waist and wait while the waves rise higher and all around and we will lift we will wash and water the water is all around and up upon your shoulders now?'

They shrugged, and they laughed, and they came to a standstill.

'Can you, fucking, sorry, can you speak more slowly, please?'

'Oh yes! That's right. That's right.'

7 |

'Sssss. Sssss.'

The word was snapped in half before it even hit the air, of course. Storm. Storm. Nothing to it. The young woman telling him to take his time didn't help. Time wasn't the shortage here.

'Sssss.'

He rubbed his face, and kept at it. Repeat your transmission. Interference. Repeat.

'Sstem. Sstam. Sstaam.' Christ alive.

'Stand? Standing?'

'No. Sstaarm.' The difficulty in just having his mouth make the right shape, even when he knew the actual word. Which was not always by any long stretch of the means.

'Are you saying *storm*, Robert?'

'Yes, well obviously, yes. Ssstorm.' Bingo, lady. Roger that.

'There was a storm?'

'Yes. Sstorm. Obviously. No storm, no storm. Bang! Bang! Storm come come. Phew! Storm!'

The young woman was standing beside him while he tried to speak. The chairs all pushed to one end of the room and everyone watching. Amira there was calling questions.

'Did the storm come suddenly, Robert?'

Rachel clapped her hands, sharp. The noise like a crack. He looked at her. He was right back at Station K. now, on top of Priestley Head, watching the weather come charging in towards them. That moment when he knew it would hit hard. Bracing himself. That moment when he knew he had mistaked in leaving the other two on their own. Not mistaked. Miss. Calc. Miscal. Mistook.

'Yes, yes, of course. More. More sudden. Big storm. Bang!'

Rachel took a chair, and banged on the seat. Mary yelped in surprise. He waved a hand in front of his face.

'Bang! Bang! No storm, now storm come, bang! Christ!'

He staggered backwards, reeling from the force of the wind. Rachel pulled a table into the middle of the room, and looked at him expectantly. He didn't know what she expected. He was close to the edge of the cliff. One more blast of wind and he'd be knocked all the way over. His radio wasn't working. He'd let Thomas go out on the ice.

'Tell us that again, Robert?'

'No storm. Sky, sky. Bang!'

As he said *bang*, Rachel flipped the table suddenly onto its side. There was a silence in the room, and then uproar.

'Oh that's right, very very good, that's right!'

'No no no, fuck, that's the one it is!'

Robert watched their responses. He had a feeling he didn't know the name for.

'Ha! Christ!' They wanted to know more. Continue the debrief. Repeat the transmission. 'Yes! Big storm. Bang! Storm!'

'Okay, so a storm came, suddenly?'

'Yes, yes, of course.'

'And before the storm; was it cold already?'

'Ha! Ha! Code. Code. Ant–ant. Code.'

He always had to reach for the words. As though they'd been put on a high shelf in the stores. Out of reach. Or left outside, snowed under, needing to be dug out. He used his hands to fill in the gaps, when he couldn't quite get to the words. The woman had helped him with this. Liz. Show us, Robert. Use anything.

He rubbed his arms, and shivered from the cold. He pointed to the ground, to the south, all the way down there: Antarctica.

'But you were wearing special clothes, to help you cope with the cold?'

'Yes, obviously, yes.'

'What were you wearing, Robert? Can you show us getting dressed ready for going outside on the base?'

That moment when he knew he had missed. Mistook. Got it wrong. When he knew he had to fix it before anyone found out. Found him out.

|

He went back to his seat and sat down. He closed his eyes. For a moment Amira thought he was withdrawing. There was a pause while the rest of the group watched to see how she would react. He had sometimes been a reluctant participant. He was suspicious of activities without a clear goal. Amira could imagine him using words like *impractical* or *inconsequential*, if he could access those words. She had been surprised that he'd kept coming to the meetings, after walking out of the first two. She waited. Mary was talking softly.

Robert opened his eyes, yawned, stretched his arms, and rubbed his face. There was a shine in his eyes that she hadn't seen before. Something like playfulness, or an enjoyment in his own playfulness. The sheer unfamiliarity of it. He stood, still stretching, and launched into a long mime of getting dressed, standing on one leg to pull on his imaginary pants, with Wiktor suddenly reaching out his one strong arm for support. There was a general chatter of encouragement in the room. Rachel began to lightly mirror his actions: pulling on vests and fleeces, zipping up overcoats, tugging on thick gloves. When he was done, he staggered across the room, his movements thickened now by the imaginary layers, not by his stroke. He reached for a door, Rachel by his side, and as they both yanked it open they staggered backwards with the impact of the icy southern wind. Together they walked out to face it, and the group went with them, picturing now the steel grey skies, the shrouded horizon, the icebergs turning distantly in the bay. The ice crunching and slipping beneath their boots. The force of the wind against them, and the sluggish clumsiness of their hands inside the thick gloves, struggling with the straps and fastenings on the supply sled. As Rachel ploughed ahead into the coming storm, Robert tapped her on the shoulder. She turned to him, curiously, hovering between staying in the role and slipping out of it.

'Ssss. Ssstop.'

She waited, and he gestured behind them.

'Door!'

She stepped back, and closed the door securely, and the two of them waded on through the storm, on towards the distant safety of the coffee machine and the biscuits.

|

The talk of a show came slowly over the next few weeks. Amira put bits of the story together, and the dancers worked through the same movements again and again. Shall we try that one more time? We could have the audience sitting here? The word *audience* was slipped out casually, as though she was hoping they wouldn't notice. But there were more, and they did. *Audience. Stage. Lights. Rehearsal.* She's fucking sorry what is it she's fucking joking now she must be. Oh yes that's true, that's right. But she told them they'd come a long way together and it would be nice, wouldn't it, to share what they'd done? It need only be family to start off with, family and friends and one or two others. It need only be a small thing.

Wiktor brought a laptop to the meetings and put together some images for a back projection. Pictures, maps, simple texts. He talked, slowly, about lighting and about sound effects. Mary made it clear she wanted to take part. When she read from the page she could speak clearly. Sean finally agreed to sing. Peter said he would stand by the door and wash away the tide of all the floating in upon the shore of us where we become the who you are and here you are you see you know and there to the chair you go you know, and it was agreed that this was a job he could do well.

Amira tried to take elements from everyone's stories. Mary's horse racing was in there, and Raymond's accident on the building site. Sean had a complicated story about a Frank Sinatra lookalike competition; they'd never really got to the bottom of it, but it gave him a chance to sing. Robert's story was the framework for everything, however. Everyone's story is important, she assured them. But we love a howling gale and a bit of drama, don't we?

There were nerves, and changes of heart, and some shouting. People became distracted. But Amira set a date, the other side of Christmas, and they talked about who they would like to be there, and together they worked on sending out invitations. They carried on working towards it. She called it a *sharing*, to take the pressure off. This didn't make it any easier.

|

'And you didn't know where the other two were?'

'Oh! That's right!'

'Robert?'

There was a question. She was asking him a question again. What was she asking him? There was the storm, and the battle to get back down from the edge of the cliff. The radio, and the silence. The white noise.

'Gone. Gone. All white,' he said. 'See, see. See nothing. Storm.' This wasn't enough. He wasn't saying enough. He wasn't making it clear.

'So. You got back to the hut, and you got inside, is that right?'

The young woman was talking quietly and the whole room was quiet. He nodded. He had come through the door and forced the door shut. The sound of the storm was muffled. He was standing in the middle of the circle, his head bowed and his hands on his thighs. He needed to get out of the wet-weather gear. He needed to get to the radio. His struggles through the storm had left him shattered and short of breath. There had been a pain in his head that he knew for a bad sign.

'You must be exhausted now. You must be relieved to be back in a safe place.'

'Yes, yes. He must be. He must be.'

'And this would be when you radioed for help, was it?'

'Ex, ex, sausted, yes.'

'Can you show us the radio? Working the radio?'

The radio was a long way off. He would be held responsible. He shouldn't have gone off to Priestley Head like that, leaving the two lads behind. He needed to resolve this situation for himself. There would be trouble. They would be back soon. The storm would clear and they would resolve. They would return. There was no need. The radio. He had to get out of this. There was a pain in his head. That he knew for a bad. The cold was glass against his face.

The young woman was there. She slipped a hand around his waist. There was the radio there. Don't use the radio. Resolve this situation before anyone. Say the radio broken. She led him back towards his seat. There was Luke, coming out of the storm without Thomas. There was that look on his face. Stand by for a brief quickening. Situation upstate.

He closed his eyes for a moment, trying to find his sense of balance. There was something he needed to say. The chair was very close. When he opened his eyes he was leaning towards it. The young woman was there.

'Sstorm. And no storm. Bang quiet, quiet.' There was something he needed to say. He looked around. The young woman was there. He kept leaning. She moved towards him. He leaned until he was falling, and then he fell.

8 |

Anna spent the afternoon barrowing thick layers of mulch to the vegetable beds and fruit cages. She had been turning the pile all through the autumn, and the decaying leaves were full of worms and beetles and all manner of microbia. The just-right smell of it was an immense pleasure. The bright green nubs of snowdrops and crocuses were nudging through the soil. There was time to finish off out here, before they had to go.

Sara was in the house with Robert. She had booked time off work for this. She had been struck by something she'd seen when she'd taken Robert to the group. He was really committed, was the most she could say. It was difficult to explain.

Anna spread the mulch across the last bed, working it around the broad beans. They'd been in since the early autumn, and their growth had stalled. They were biding their time. The fruit trees were cracking their first buds. The air was clear, with just an edge of dampness coming up from the fields and drains beyond the end of the garden. In the fields, the winter wheat was coming through.

She still didn't quite understand what it was they'd been invited to. It's a performance, is it? Bridget asked, and she said that no, they'd been told it wasn't a performance; the invitation calls it a *sharing*. Robert's calling it a dress rehearsal. Sara says they've been working with dancers, but they're not dancing. Bridget had given her a look that was hard to read, and said she didn't think Tim would ever have worked with dancers, had he made it back. Anna told her that there were several differences between Tim and Robert, in fact, weren't there? Bridget had stopped talking for a while.

If Robert was anxious about the *showing* then he was hiding it well. When she asked him about it, he looked distracted and said it was good, of course, obviously, it was good. This was not information. She asked him what would happen in the showing; what would he be doing? He waved a hand in front of his face: he couldn't say. Whether he didn't have the words or he didn't want to use them was impossible to tell, now.

|

Outside the centre they saw Luke. He was waiting for something. Anna didn't understand why he was there. Sara walked ahead quickly and was the first to reach him. She said something Anna couldn't hear and he smiled. She touched his arm. He dipped his head and then he looked over her shoulder towards them.

'What's up, Doc?'

'Loo, loo. Luke.' They shook hands. Robert kept hold of Luke's hand for a long moment. 'Luke. Well, obviously. Ha! Okay.'

'You all set then, Doc? Sara says you've been working hard on this. Something new for you, isn't it?'

'Obviously, obviously. Nothing. Small thing. Okay. Okay. In, now. In.' He started heading towards the door. The showing wasn't due to start for an hour but he needed to prepare. Sara suggested that Anna could take him inside. She would go for a coffee and come back, she said. Luke could come with her, if he liked? They would come back when it was time for the show. Luke said that would work. He was talking to Anna when he said it, but looking at Sara. That would definitely work. There was a question Anna wanted to ask, but Robert was already inside the centre and waiting by the lift.

When they got to the room Amira looked at Anna and said they wouldn't be starting for a while. Anna asked if there was anything she could do to help, and Amira said thank you, no, and turned away. She called across the room to ask about lights. Robert was already talking to one of the young dancers who were not dancers. She was dressed all in white. She was watching him intently, and nodding. In the corner of the room the other two dancers who were not dancers were also dressed in white. They were stretching. Anna found a chair at the back of the room and sat down.

Somebody was standing on a chair by the windows, sticking black paper to the glass. The sheets kept peeling off and floating to the floor, and he kept swearing loudly. A man she recognised was crouching next to a projector, fiddling with leads and peering up at the screen behind him. It was Wiktor. The screen was blue, with the words *NO SOURCE DETECTED* running across the middle. He kept doing something different with the leads, and looking at the screen again.

Mary was sitting in her wheelchair not far from Anna, reading quietly from a sheet of paper. She was dressed very elegantly, and

262

her hair had been freshly done. She looked up at Anna and smiled.

'Went the wefted warp we came around,' she said. Anna looked at her, trying to make the words make sense.

'I'm sorry?' she said.

'Once upon a time,' Mary said again, nodding firmly. Anna smiled.

'I'm looking forward to seeing this,' she told Mary.

There was a cracking sound from the loudspeakers, and a loud blast of white noise. Wiktor looked up from the projector and apologised, and people put their hands over their ears. The white noise vanished, and a picture appeared on the screen. It was a picture of Robert, outside the red field hut at Station K. Anna looked for him in the room. She didn't know why there was a picture of him on the screen. He was talking to the man Anna remembered as Raymond. There was a look on his face that she recognised. She'd seen it when he'd been at conferences or Institute events, in rooms full of people talking and holding cups of coffee. Rooms like this, but bigger, and busier. It was the look he had when he'd been fully engrossed in what he was doing. When he hadn't needed her to be there.

By the time Sara and Luke arrived, Peter was at the door giving people handouts. They brought one over to her, and Sara asked why she was sitting right at the back. The handouts explained why the group had started meeting, and what they had been trying to achieve. Aphasia affects all aspects of a person's communication but the ability to tell stories can be a significant loss. Your loved one might struggle to talk about their day, or to tell grandchildren about key events in their lives. We have been exploring ways of telling stories with all the tools available. The logos of several funding organisations took up most of the back page, that of the university prominent among them. The language was rather affected, Anna felt. *Loved one* was an assumption, for a start.

When it started, there were a lot of people in the room. There weren't even enough chairs. Sara and Luke were talking beside her, but she couldn't catch what they said. Amira gathered everyone's attention, and said most of the things that were already written on the handouts. She thanked all the funding organisations, and all the people in the group. The lights went off, and a popping noise came from the speakers. Wiktor apologised, and did something with the leads, and in the half-light she saw Robert make his way to the middle of the stage.

|

It started with darkness. The room dark and bare. Robert hunched over a table, or a desk. A soft white light behind him. A beeping sound. Long and short notes, over and over. The light brightened. It became clearer that Robert was working a Morse code machine, one finger on the keypad: tap-tap-tap, tip-tip-tip, tap-tap-tap.

He was dressed in coats and hoods and gloves. He kept his eyes down, and worked the machine. Everyone was very quiet, watching him. Waiting for what would come next. A line of dots and dashes moved across a screen behind him. He lowered his hood with one hand and looked up at the audience.

'My name. Is. Robert. I am expo guy. Expo, guide.'

They knew the word before he said it. They said the word *expedition* for him in their heads, willing the word into the air, the tricksy fucking word it is, bring it out now, ex, expo, *expedition*. *Expedition Guide*.

'I am guide. Assist. Ah. Ah! I support walk, long walk, travel!'

There was laughter in the room again. Oh, that's right, very good, go round. Go around the word. Wiktor made some small adjustments on his laptop and the screen behind Robert brightened until he became a silhouette against it. He stood, slowly, levering himself up with his stick, and held out one arm.

'My name. Is Robert. I am. Guide. Explore. I had stroke. I had a, I have a, aphasia. I am. Tech. Guide. I work. Ant, ant, ant.'

There was more laughter. The impossible word, the tricksy fucking word, they had never heard him say it and still he kept on trying. Wiktor put a map on the screen behind Robert: a map of the world, sliding south from Europe and zooming in as it reached the Antarctic Circle and the horned white splodge of Antarctica. Robert pointed to the map behind him.

'Here! I work here. Is cold. Is very cold.'

He wrapped his arms around himself, huddled against the memory of weather. They all felt the cold with him. Brrr, brrr, that's right, Robert. Very cold. They were trying not to talk out loud. But they wanted him to know they were there. Carry on, Robert. You can. You can do it.

'I work. I work long time. In. Ant, ant.'

He pointed to the map again.

'Many years. Young man, old man. Many stories. This. This story. One day. Working. Storm comes.'

He tipped his head to one side, and arranged his face into a fearful expression, as though he could hear something coming.

'Oh yes, that's right, Robert, watch out!'

'Sshh. Sshh.'

'Big storm come. Come quick!'

With one arm he lifted the back edge of the desk and tipped it forwards, sending it crashing to the floor. The lights flashed on and off, and there was a noise like a howling gale. There were gasps and shouts of surprise. Half the people in the room were not actually surprised, but the noise was so sudden that they shouted anyway. Oh yes, very good, very good. Went the water where we were. The white light kept flashing and the storm sounds got louder. Robert was kneeling low behind the table, shielding from the weather. He pushed against it with his shoulder, turning it to one side. It looked like hard work. Come on Robert, come on. You can. Come on. Once he had turned the table right around, the storm sounds stopped. The room was quiet. They could hear Robert breathing. Gasping.

'When storm hit. When the storm hit. Sudden. Bang! Bang! Here. My knees. Storm come. Push. Push me. To my knees.'

Amira was standing by the door, watching all this. She was holding the script, and mouthing the words. The script is not the script, she had told them. Use the words you find, in the moment. The words in the script are just signposts. Robert was finding his own way there, going around, going the long way around. When the storm. When the storm hits. Amira looked surprised, or concerned. She looked as though she didn't understand how this had all come together. The tricksy fucking gang of them all. Six months of meeting in a room, and they'd got to this. It wasn't feasible.

The lights went low, and in the darkness one of the dancers came and helped Robert back to his seat. The table was moved away. And as the lights came back up the audience saw Mary, wheeled to the middle of the floor by Gavin, the dancer, dressed in white. There was a spotlight on her, and the room settled into a hush, waiting. She held a piece of paper, and slowly read from it. When she read, she spoke clearly, and people no longer looked at her in that vague way they sometimes did. She lifted a hand to say: wait, now hear this.

'Once. Upon a – time. Our stories. Were told. In – words.'

'Mary! Very good, very good, that's right Mary, tell your words now, sorry but that's right!'

'Now we talk. We talk in – new ways.'

There was applause, and shouting, and people telling each other to hush and listen.

Each one of them had a turn. Mary talked about horse racing, and about early mornings working with the trainers on the Downs. Sean talked about working in pubs, and sang unaccompanied. Raymond held up his hands and told the shocking story of his accident. There were images on the screen to add context. There was clapping, and shouting, and people telling other people to hush again.

Robert came back for the closing moment, standing and leaning into the sound effects of the storm. The sounds got louder, and he swayed and staggered in the wind. Rachel stood close to him, echoing his movements. He put his hand over his eyes, shielding them from the sun, and he searched the horizon. He took a radio from his pocket and held it up to his mouth. The sound effects changed to the hissing white noise of radio interference.

'This – Doc. Hello? Hello? Christ. Now. Hear – me? Hear – me? Over.'

He leaned backwards and he kept on leaning. He fell, and Rachel was right there to hold him; to catch him, and lower him down to the floor. The lights dimmed, and she was still lowering him slowly to the floor.

There was quiet, and then some clapping, and then an eruption of clapping and shouting, the noise almost like a roaring wind, or the broken hiss of white noise.

|

The applause at the end was louder than she'd expected, given the number of people in the room. People stood if they could, and added their voices to the sound of the applause. Sara was trying to say something, and put an arm around her waist. Beside Sara, Luke paused his clapping and steepled his hands around his nose and mouth. There was a lot of noise in the room.

She realised that she was supposed to feel excitement and satisfaction. She mostly felt a great sadness. It was the kind of sadness that felt oddly appropriate. There was some permission in it. It was difficult to put into words.

She had only ever wanted him to come back from Antarctica in one piece. And he had come home but he was different. Your loved one may not be the same as the person they were before. Your loved one will still be. The group's activities are designed to encourage. We have been working together on these stories for several weeks and we would like to share them with you now. We have some things we would like to say.

He had come back.

The light was bright in the room and Robert was looking towards her. There were people moving around between them. He was blinking as though he couldn't quite see. He put a hand over his eyes to shield them. She lifted her hand to find his attention. He lifted his hand to wave.

There were ripples on the water. The ice slipped and broke into the sea. The daylight was silence across the Sound. Behind the mountains, the darker clouds gathered.

A storm moved through the valley.

In the distance the field hut swayed and shuddered on its footings, the heavy canvas straps straining to hold it down. Inside, the timber panelling creaked and the oil-fired stove roared. The beds were empty. A chair was overturned. The lights on the radio blinked on and off.

The light dimmed and brightened again. A bank of cloud blew in. An area of high pressure stilled the air. Water vapour froze in the air and crystallised and the snow settled slowly against the flanks of the mountains, across the ridges on either side of the bay, falling deep inside the crevasses that ran jaggedly out from the sides of the glacier as it pushed on down to the sea.

At the foot of Priestley Head, beside a damaged skidoo, a small orange tent was gradually submerged by the snow.

Time passed.

Radio signals passed occasionally through the air.

In the orange tent, a body breathed.

The weather stilled.

Time was passing, or had already passed. There was movement inside the tent. Rustling and puffing and the sharp relief of a zip.

The man hauled himself out onto the snow.

The colour of the light on the water was steel, silver, scour, scattered by each beaten indentation on the surface, each eddy of wind or swirl of current.

The man was bright and red and large against the fresh white snow.

There was a great sound and nothing. A calm overcame him.

He sat, and he waited.

The calm came over him.

Silence, and distance. An immense sense of space.

Something was wrong.

He felt it unlikely that he would survive and yet he knew with certainty that everything would be fine. Everything would be right, and had always been right.

The feeling of rightness was a thick, solid feeling. It was tangible, he would try to explain, later. He felt a part of everything surrounding. Everything surrounding felt a part of him.

It was difficult to put into words, he would try to say.

His lack of words was so absolute that he couldn't quite fathom what was lost.

There was no experience of loss. There was only the silence of his own brain, and the silence was a tremendous relief.

He sat, and he watched, and he breathed.

His breathing was the outline of the mountain ridges. Crisp white against the soft blue sky. The slow peaks and the sudden falls. Up, up, down. In, out.

He sat. And he watched. And he was.

His blood pulsed through his body as he breathed. His breathing was the dip and the surge of seawater breaking against the edge of the ice. The water moved against the ice, and his blood washed in and out of his hands. His breathing traced each crest and gully along the mountain ridge. His breath clouded in front of him, and the clouds billowed up into the bare blue sky and were swept northward into weather fronts along the coast.

The cells of his body and the crystals of the snow.

The clouds of his breath and the clouds across the bare blue sky.

There were scraps and artefacts in his vision. They swam and shimmered before him.

He took off his gloves to look at the blood moving in his fingers.

He knew help would come. He knew his body was failing. He knew he was damaged. He knew it would be okay.

He knew all these things.

There was a noise from the radio in the snow beside him. The noise was talking but he didn't know the words. It didn't seem important now. The noise repeated, and repeated.

There was somewhere he needed to be.

He stood. It took a long time. He walked.

His body was leaning over to one side. He fell.

He waited. There was somewhere he needed to be.

He knew.

He knew all these things as a trembling in the centre of his chest; a droning remote and deep within him.

Something was come.

He didn't know his own name. He couldn't bring to mind the people who would miss him when he didn't get home.

The droning became louder, and more vivid.

He didn't know what a home was, or a person.

He stood and he walked and he fell.

He waited. He stood. The word *ice* was suddenly important. The word *scrape*.

From somewhere beyond the cliffs there was a billow of blue smoke and the billow drifted away.

He closed his eyes.

There was a droning sensation in the middle of his chest; in his head.

There was something he was supposed to have done.

The droning took on a sense of direction.

It didn't seem important any more.

In the far distance the droning sound took the shape of a red aeroplane, small and slow, barely moving towards him.

A blown and flimsy scrap of red.

A faint noise from the radio, like distant applause.

The grey sea and the white mountains and the small red scrap of an aeroplane blown across the ice towards him.

The thought of moving his body and the thought drifting away.

The red plane small come bigger now.

He didn't even know the word for red, but he knew this was the small far-off beginning of something new.

Acknowledgements

In 2004, I travelled to Antarctica as part of the Writers & Artists Programme run by the British Antarctic Survey, supported by Arts Council England. I am grateful to all involved in making that possible, and in particular to the late David Walton for doing so much to develop the programme.

More recently, I benefitted from the assistance of Joanna Rae and Ieuan Hopkins at the BAS Archives Service, and in particular that of Mike Dinn, from the BAS Medical Unit, who was generous with his time

It should be noted that the 'Antarctic Research Institute' featured in this novel is a fictional organisation.

While learning about stroke and aphasia, I benefitted greatly from the experience and insight of Grace Rowley, Clare Sedgwick, Sally Knapp, Professor Nikola Sprigg, Beth Newell, Jackie Farmer, Hazel Warren, and Sarah Marriot, all of whom shared their time and knowledge generously. Books by Becky Moss, Bridget Long, Carole Pound, Caroline Firenza, Celia Woolf, Chris Ireland, Jayne Lindsay, Jill Bolte Taylor, Robert McCrum, Sally Byng, Sheila Hale, Sue Gilpin, and Susie Parr were also helpful; as was the work of Rosetta Life, and their performance of *Stroke Odysseys*.

I spent several months as a regular guest of the Aphasia Nottingham self-help group, and am grateful for the welcome I was shown by everyone there, and for how much I was taught. I hope I have repaid your trust, and I'm sorry I kept winning the quiz.

Thanks are also due, for several reasons, to: Andy Stevenson-Jones, Benjamin Johncock, Chloe Hooper, Chris Gribble (and the National Centre for Writing), Chris Power, Dan Suri, Darren Chetty, Éireann Lorsung, Emilio Costa, Jenn Ashworth, Melissa Harrison, Mel O'Neill, Ruth Mottram, Sarah Hall, and my colleagues at the University of Nottingham.

Thanks to everyone at 4th Estate who turned this into a book, including Helen Garnons-Williams, Marigold Atkey, Amber Burlinson, Saba Ahmed, Chris Gurney, Graham Holmes, Julian Humphries, Matt Clacher, and Michelle Kane.

Thanks to Tracy Bohan and Jin Auh, and all at the Wylie Agency.

Most of all, thanks to Rosie, and to E, L, D, L, and A, for getting us through 2020 in one piece.